Also by Lance C Wilson

THE LAIRD OF BRAIDWOOD
Historical

TEARS OVER THE KIMBERLEYS

DARE TO LIVE THE DREAM

THE CHILDREN OF KIMBERLEY COTTAGE
BILLY OF THE NORTH
MY FIELD OF DREAMS

THE STONE PEOPLE

DARK SIDE OF THE ROCK

THE GULF

PAULINE'S JOURNEY

FIFTY ACHES & PAINS

A satirical look at senior citizen sex

LANCE C WILSON

Copyright © 2016 Lance C Wilson

Printed and published by Kimberley Cottage Publishing

This is a work of Adult Fiction.

All characters and events are portrayed fictitiously.

National Library of Australia Cataloguing-in-Publication entry:

Author: Wilson, Lance C, 1945

Titles: Fifty Aches & Pains and Meg's Story

Editor: Rhonda Scott JP

Cover photos, design and layout by Alan Jennison

ISBN: 9780 – 977 – 550 – 562

Dewey No. A 823.4

A CiP record for this book is available from the National Library of Australia

Many thanks

I must in particular thank my Editor, Rhonda Scott for the many hours spent sitting at her desk, working without complaint in an untiring effort to complete my last three books, including these two stories.

Many thanks too to Alan Jennison for producing such wonderful, innovative covers for the three books and making them print ready.

and

As always, special thanks to my wife Cynthia for her constant support and assistance.

Foreword

Join Beryl and Merle, two widows who decide on the spur of the moment to have one last fling, both pensioners living in a retirement village for several years and finding it increasingly difficult to stretch their budgets. A big event for them was Bingo night at the local club and afterwards a ten-dollar flutter on the pokies.

Neither had many friends and although theirs was a caustic friendship in many ways, they relied on each other for company. Despite both having children, visits by their offspring were few and far between. Loneliness was the catalyst for the relationship and over the years it prospered even though their beliefs differed and they disagreed on many issues.

The only real things they had in common were that they each had long marriages and both husbands had succumbed to illness in their early sixties, leaving them confused and lonely widows. They had then sold their family homes and moved into the village, mainly for the sake of security and for the company of other retirees. After purchasing their new units neither had a great deal of finance left so had to be frugal with money, their earning capacity was zero and the pension their only future income.

Although not grossly overweight, they were each carrying a few extra kilos, had high blood pressure and problems with cholesterol. Combined with the effects of medication and their joint stiffness, causing more than a few aches and pains, many a conversation was about their ailments. No one else seemed interested as they sat in the club gossiping and moaning about their disabilities so they listened intently to each other, trying to show some compassion.

This changed when the only win they ever had on the pokies, after far too many gin and tonics, resulted in a bet to find romance on the internet!

Chapter One

Beryl Jones fussed about in front of her bedroom mirror, it was Thursday night, Bingo night. All week she had looked forward to the event, it was her only break from the unit, apart from a short trip once a week to the grocery store. Beryl felt excited, she would meet up with her friend Merle White, enjoy a cheap meal before Bingo, and have her usual flutter on the pokies. Gazing at the mirror she nodded in approval.

Last week she had purchased a new dress while on her shopping expedition and although it had strained her tight budget she felt more than happy with the purchase. For once she felt attractive, even her friend Merle commented at the time on what a difference the new garment made to her appearance. 'Yes', for some reason, Beryl felt confident tonight.

While in the city looking for the new dress Beryl was browsing in a bookshop for something to read and found a novel titled *'Dare to Live the Dream'*. It too was about an elderly woman living in a retirement village, who through a series of events found love again. Although racy, the novel appealed to Beryl, 'Perhaps,' she thought, 'at my age maybe I don't need to live such a sedate and predictable life, just waiting to die like most of the other village residents.'

Closing the door she stopped, 'It was a little chilly tonight,' she mused, 'maybe I should get my coat', then shaking her head, decided to go as she was. Her coat was old and dowdy, well past its use-by-date, so 'why cover her new dress?' she thought. Walking briskly, she came to her friend's door and knocked, Merle opened it at once, just as anxious to get going on their night out.

"For heaven's sake Beryl, you'll freeze in that outfit," Merle told her, sarcastically as usual. "Come on Merle, it's not that far to the corner and we'll be able to get a taxi there, it's not too bad," Beryl replied, willing herself not to allow Merle to spoil the one night a week she really enjoyed.

"Come on then or we'll be late. I hope no one thinks you're a hooker, flashing so much on a cold night," Merle shot back. "Actually Merle, if someone tried to pick us up I would be chuffed to think we looked so bloody sexy!" Beryl laughed, trying to lighten the mood.

"I don't suppose it makes any difference. Neither of us would bring in much nowadays anyway, but there was a time Beryl let me tell you, when the men stared at me wherever I went!" Merle remarked, always having to have the last word.

Luckily a cab was waiting on the taxi rank and the driver, a young Indian man, had taken them before. Jumping out, he bowed as he held the rear door open and welcomed them, smiling, "Good evening ladies."

Merle ignored his pleasantries, instead loudly criticising taxi drivers in general for ripping off old ladies, hardly having finished her rant as they pulled up outside the club. The young man just nodded in agreement with Merle, still lecturing him as he jumped out and held the door open for them. It was a quiet night and he was willing to suffer the lecture. Still smiling, he happily pocketed the fare.

Entering the venue they found the room already half-full, so first up purchased their raffle tickets for the meat and grocery hampers. Last week Merle had won and they had each enjoyed a week of lamb and beef, instead of sausages of dubious quality, or chicken which usually gave them the trots because of the growth hormones and antibiotics forced into them.

Finding seats, Merle sat down while Beryl made her way to the bar for the first of the two drinks they would consume that night. It was a practiced ritual and Merle would buy their second drinks during the half-time break. Returning, Beryl placed the drinks on the table and they began acknowledging the many players. There were a few from their village and bus loads from elsewhere. Tonight was a big night as the prize had jackpotted to one thousand dollars, the biggest ever and the tension and excitement was building, with only ten minutes to go before the games commenced.

One player in a wheelchair, speeding to her seat nearly knocked Merle over in her rush. Not even apologising, she reversed and sped off leaving a shocked and fuming Merle dusting herself off and shuffling the chair back into position. Beryl knew not to say anything to inflame the situation and tried to change the subject before any trouble started.

"Oh, here comes Jean Brown and her new partner. Rosie Kelly told me last week she had met someone on-line, on one of those dating sites or something," Beryl told Merle, who was huffing and puffing, fit to kill.

"Don't bloody care! Look at the grinning old tart, dressed up like a lamb when she's mutton, and scrawny at that! Shit, she's coming this way," uttered Merle.

"Hi folks," Jean crooned, smelling like a perfume store, "can we sit with you two please? I usually

11

sit with Roma and the girls but they only have one seat and I don't want to be parted from my Henry." "No problems Jean, nice to meet you Henry. I am Beryl and this is my friend Merle who has just been rammed by a runaway wheel-chair," Beryl stood up and waved to the two vacant seats at their table, like royalty waving to a crowd.

Merle nodded in recognition at the smiling Jean but was still fuming and looked like a rattlesnake about to strike. Beryl couldn't help noticing Jean was constantly rolling her eyes at her new man, who in turn seemed to drool over the besotted Jean.

"Can I get you girls a drink before the raffles start?" a friendly Henry asked as he rose from his seat. Bending over he gave Jean a peck on the cheek and, not unnoticed by Beryl, had a little squeeze of her left tit!

"Thank you," Merle purred, the offer of a free drink immediately changing her demeanour. Beryl, having seen how all Merle's inhibitions seemed to disappear after a few drinks, actually thought, 'A few more and she's yours, Henry old boy.'

Henry returned just as the first game began. The three women played intently but Beryl noticed Henry had missed a few games. Obviously bored he took on the position of drinks supplier, keeping the glasses of all three Bingo players constantly filled and as the game progressed the camaraderie at the table increased due to the effects of the alcohol consumed.

The main game offering the major prize commenced and at this point of the proceedings no one at the table had won anything, even in any of the several raffle draws.

Beryl realised that, having filled her card after marking it at each call, she had won but was so overcome with disbelief, when she put her hand up to yell 'Bingo', nothing came out. Luckily Henry, who was standing behind, saw her dilemma and yelled it out for her. Stunned by her win Beryl found it hard to stand up but Henry helped her make her way to the stage to collect the prize amid loud clapping and cheering from the crowd.

Merle sat livid. It had always been she who had won any prizes, but now all the attention was on Beryl, looking resplendent in her new dress and being assisted by Henry. Even she had to admit he was a fine looking man, 'God knows how scrawny old Jean had got her claws into him' she thought.

Beryl was overwhelmed at her luck. She returned to the table, counted out half of the winnings and passed it to Merle, who sat stunned at the gesture.

"We always share our winnings," an excited Beryl told her.

"Yes, but that was only a few bloody lamb chops, for fuck's sake!" an emotional Merle replied.

"No matter Merle, you shared, so it's only fair I share with you," Beryl countered.

"Tell you what, after this, let me take you out for a midnight feast to celebrate," Henry interceded.

"No, we can pay now, no need for you to Henry, but a midnight feast would be nice for once," Beryl said.

"No way, you are my guests, I have plenty of funds actually and no family to leave them to, so you will all be my guests. I'm just happy to be here, meeting Jean has changed my life," Henry replied adamantly.

Finishing the game, now all half pissed, they gathered up their belongings and Henry hailed a taxi, giving the driver instructions. They found themselves at the Casino and as they were admiring the opulent surroundings Henry guided them to a classy restaurant. Beryl knew that she and Merle and possibly Jean had never been to such a place before in their lives. As the waiter seated them and passed out menus, Henry ordered champagne and Beryl watched in awe as several bottles were delivered to their table. When Henry had tasted and nodded his approval at the waiter, the champagne was poured for each of them.

Henry excused himself and made his way to the rest room. Merle now on a high, not sipping but guzzling the champagne, looked at Jean, "You have a catch there Jean, how did you meet him?" she asked, pointing at Henry as he was leaving.

"Well, to be honest, girls," Jean replied, unable to hide her triumph like that of a cat coming out of a dairy, "I joined a dating site for seniors on the internet. It was one of those naughty sites actually!"

"What do you mean, 'naughty sites'?" Merle quizzed, now totally interested.

"You know, we exchange naughty messages," Jean giggled.

"No actually I don't know. Do you mean sex messages?" Merle continued quizzing.

"Yep, I suppose at our age, why beat around the bush?" Jean responded.

"Hell, I thought older men our age would be unable to

14

get it up," Merle, now on a roll, quizzed again.

"That's what most people think but I am having better and longer sex now than ever in my life," Jean replied, smiling.

"You are kidding right! You mean you have good bonking sessions?" Merle fired back.

"Listen Merle, Henry can go for it three times a night and sometimes during the day, I never knew sex could be so great! I know he takes Viagra but boy does it work, he has a one-hour-turnaround!" Jean, knowing Merle was jealous, held nothing back.

Beryl sat listening intently. She had always enjoyed her intimate moments but as married life rolled along those moments became fewer and less intense. For her to find a catch like Henry would be very difficult and almost certainly impossible in her village where there was only one male and all the rest women.

Henry returned to the table and the subject was dropped. Beryl was not really that hungry but enjoyed the wonderful meal and company. She and Merle agreed at around 2am on the way home in the taxi paid for by Henry, that it was the latest either of them had stayed out for many years.

Merle suggested a late night coffee and Beryl happily accepted. Tonight had been different, first the win and then the midnight meal with Henry and Jean, certainly outside the square and so different to their usual boring weekly routine of watching TV and doing a bit of gardening to fill the days.

Beryl felt a little woozy alighting from the taxi, having drunk more that evening than ever before in her life. She knew Merle was also finding it hard to stop swaying because of having imbibed too much alcohol. Like two teenagers, they both got the giggles as Merle fumbled for the key, laughing hysterically as she finally found it but hit the door several times trying to find the keyhole. "Za bloody door is moving Beryl," she slurred.

"You're pissed Merle, all that bloody talk about other people and we are ourselves no better than two drunken old tarts," Beryl replied.

"Got it!" as she managed to open the door, "Just in time, I'm busting for a pee!" Merle laughed.

Both raced to the toilet, Beryl plonking on the seat, sighing as a gush hit the water and as she was swaying about, trying to pull her pants up, Merle pushed her aside. Unable to control herself Merle sprayed pee everywhere as she fell onto the seat, laughing uncontrollably.

Beryl made her way to the kitchen switching on the kettle to prepare two strong coffees, aware headaches were inevitable. Merle appeared in her dressing gown, "God I really must be drunk! I've pissed on myself and all over the bathroom floor but what the hell, have we had a good night or what?"

"For sure but we're not going to have such a great morning I'm afraid, we are going to have hangovers," Beryl replied.

"Listen Beryl, if bloody scraggy old Jean can get a good shagging, why can't we?" Merle slurred.

"You know Merle, I wondered the same thing. I had thought we were a bit old for that but I've been reading a book '*Dare to Live the Dream*' and it got me thinking a bit," Beryl replied.

"Are you kidding me? A friend lent me that book and I tell you what Beryl, I'm going on a dating site. I bet you my five hundred against your five hundred that I can get laid before you do!" Merle declared as she staggered towards Beryl with her hand out ready to shake on the bet.

"Not so sure about that Merle, how would we meet someone willing to go to bed with us?" Beryl looked shocked at Merle standing there swaying like a tree in a storm.

"Don't be such a chicken shit. I have a computer and we can use that to go online like Jean. Never thought you were such a bloody wuss Beryl, all talk and no action! Let's live outside the square once in our boring lives for fuck's sake!" Merle goaded.

"Ok you're on Merle, but only on the condition that we be totally honest with each other. It must be full intercourse, no cheating," Beryl replied as they shook hands and, now that the two had challenged each other, the bet somehow killed any further conversation.

Beryl found it hard to walk the short distance home and was glad when she fell into her bed. It was only then, with her head spinning, that the full impact of the bet hit her just as she fell into a deep sleep. Waking the next morning she found her mouth was dry and her head thumped. She made her way to the kitchen and swallowed two Panadol with a glass of water then stopped for a pee on the way back to bed, promising herself that she would never drink alcohol again.

Recalling the previous evening and the bet she had

made with Merle, her mind raced. Her first thought was that she would withdraw from the bet later in the day, if she recovered from her hangover, but then considered the ramifications of that decision. Merle would torment her constantly and so Beryl gave the matter further thought, 'Bugger Merle, I will show her.'

Beryl missed intimacy and thought 'If Jean can do it, so can I, and just to see the look on Merle's face when I introduce her to my stud, will be well worth it.' The very thought of a lover wrapping her in his arms and them having wild sex actually brought a smile to her lips and stirred up a passion long since forgotten. 'Yes,' she mused, 'I can win this bet, just like I won last night!'

Chapter Two

Beryl slept soundly, again waking with a raging thirst but happy the headache had gone and surprised to see it was 4pm.

Standing at the sink drinking more water, she decided to dress and go over to Merle's place. It hit her that Merle may have already joined a dating site and she was determined not to give her a moment's advantage. The actual challenge now excited Beryl. She was sick of watching stupid sitcoms on the television, even the news was boring and the politicians were full of spin. She often wondered how they could possibly consider the public were such imbeciles as to believe any of the crap most of them spewed. 'Yes', she thought, 'this is an opportunity to show old Merle up and perhaps, just perhaps, to find herself a 'Henry'.

Knocking on Merle's door, Beryl wondered if she may still be in bed, and unused to the battering their livers had taken from the copious influx of alcohol, she too may be suffering a hangover.

Merle answered the door still in her dressing gown, looking like crap, "Came over to use the internet if I may Merle. How are you feeling?" Beryl enquired.

"How does it look like I feel, for fuck's sake Beryl?' replied Merle, her usual happy self. Then hindering Beryl from entering, added, "Sorry, my computer is broken for some reason." Immediately Beryl knew Merle was lying and had the first advantage. She had seen the glow of the monitor through the crack in the door and drew a deep breath. Merle had declared war by blocking her from using the internet.

"No worries Merle, that at least means we can't start our competition until it's fixed. Hope you feel better soon lovey," Beryl smirked, her mind racing as she turned around to go home.

Slamming the door, Beryl almost hyperventilated. She knew she had insufficient funds to purchase a computer to go online, although she did have a phone and landline. Then like a bolt of lightning, it came to her, racing to the phone table she rummaged through her contact book. Some time back she had swapped numbers with Jean and there was a chance she may agree to give her some advice. Dialling the number, she waited with bated breath for what seemed an eternity, then Jean answered.

"Hi Jean, Beryl here, I need your advice. I will be straight up. Last night I made a bet with Merle, but admit I was drunk at the time. You see, we bet each other five hundred dollars in a competition to get laid. We were both going to join an on-line dating service but today Merle tells me her computer is broken. I know this is bullshit and that she has already been on-line. She wants to win. I haven't the money to buy a new one but thought you might know of one I could get second-hand or something? I also wondered if you could advise me on this internet dating business," Beryl blurted out without drawing breath.

Jean gave a low whistle, "That's exactly what I would've expected from Merle, hold on."

Beryl stood waiting, her heart beating fast, this was outright war and to lose was not an option. The only man living in the village seemed to be friendly with several women but didn't really show interest in anyone in particular although a few visited him for morning tea occasionally.

"Hi Beryl," Jean came back on," I just spoke to Henry and he thinks it's a great idea. He has a spare computer you can use and we'll bring it over later this evening if you like, so Merle doesn't see us visiting you."

"Super, I will get him to help me set it up on my phone line and show me how to use it." Beryl replied and asked, "Could you then Jean, help me set up on a dating site?"

"No worries, I'll even get a photo of you in your nice dress, and upload it for you, have you a service yet?" Jean enquired.

"No, but I'll get one first thing in the morning," Beryl promised. "Hold on," pause from Jean, "Henry said you can use his for the time being, he will set it up for you."

"Thanks heaps, Jean! I am determined to win this one," Beryl replied hanging up, gloating at her success.

Beryl made a small salad and sat contemplating her next move, aware that meeting men was going to be difficult because of the life she led and most of those at the club seemed to have partners. Jean was right, for the majority of single women like her a dating agency was the only hope.

Jean and Henry turned up later that evening to find Beryl traipsing up and down the dining room like a caged lion. To her, losing the bet and Merle finding a lover first,

21

was unthinkable.

Henry soon had the computer, a laptop, set up and showed her how to unplug it when Merle visited so she wouldn't know Beryl had access to the internet. Using Henry's password and under Jean's guidance, Beryl logged onto the dating site. Sure enough they found Merle's profile. She had indeed joined the site earlier that day, uploading a photo of herself taken years before in a bikini and introducing herself as a 'Fit and healthy lady, seeking partner to enjoy life with, wide range of interests'.

Henry pointed out though that she had not answered several questions, such as 'shaved' or 'natural' and 'favourite position' and added that answering these questions, as Jean had done, showed men that she was interested in a sexual relationship. Jean, as promised, took a photo of Beryl made up and in her new dress. Henry uploaded the top half of the photo revealing her breasts, telling Beryl that a recent photo would give her an advantage over Merle, whose prospects would not be impressed that she was years older than in her profile photo.

Beryl waved farewell to her helpers late that night and crashed into bed exhausted but confidant she had done her best, and satisfied at least that she was on equal footing with her adversary Merle. Waking early and checking her inbox she found only one email from a young man who promised to ride her for hours if she paid him one hundred dollars an hour for the service. She deleted the email and blocked the sender deciding that if she was to win, it had to be with someone genuine, not a paid gigolo.

On Sunday knowing Merle would drop over as usual

for morning tea, Beryl hid the laptop and prepared some cakes. On cue Merle arrived, looking far better than the last time they had met. Neither mentioned the bet but Beryl knew Merle would be trying to find out if she had taken any steps to win it. Merle too had received an email from the same young man and had thought on the subject for some time before erring on the side of caution and, like Beryl, deleting it and blocking the sender. She knew if she turned up with a younger man Beryl was smart enough to know he would be being paid for the service, since no fit young man would waste his time bonking an older woman unless it was for financial gain.

As soon as Merle left Beryl raced into the bedroom and retrieved the laptop. Logging into the site, she was elated to find that an elderly gentleman living in another state had sent her a message. Beryl replied, indicating her interest and they began to correspond. After a few days he asked if they might meet for coffee if he came to Sydney. Beryl happily agreed and named a coffee shop in the local shopping centre, considering it a safe meeting place.

Beryl met Merle at her front door again that Thursday evening before Bingo and they caught a taxi to the local club, buying tickets in the raffles and their regular two drinks on arrival. Jean and Henry had gone off on a trip for a few weeks and both women were thankful they'd avoid Henry's constant supply of alcohol. Like sparring warriors, neither admitted being on the dating site and Beryl skilfully avoided the subject, fully aware that if Merle had had any luck arranging a date she would be unable to keep it a secret until after copulation had occurred.

When Bingo was over, and with drink number two in hand, they retired to the pokies for their ritual flutter. Beryl had lost her usual enthusiasm and nervously watched Merle batting her eyelids at any male who came within range. Most being regulars returned the smile and walked on, mainly because, Beryl assumed, they had female partners with them.

Having fed the machine her last dollar Beryl didn't at first take much notice of the sound of bells ringing then turning saw she had won a jackpot! Staff came running and other gamblers stared in envy, Beryl had won three thousand dollars. Amid all the commotion Beryl had not noticed Merle return to the bar and upon receiving her prize in the form of cash from the night manager she realised she hadn't witnessed the win.

Beryl stopped, stunned upon entering the bar to find Merle sitting chatting with an elderly man. The war had truly begun and since she now had a war chest decided this time to keep her win from Merle, whom she was sure would do the same in her position.

Upon reaching the bar, in her sweetest voice Beryl said, "Hi Merle, introduce me to your friend."

"Oh ah, oh Dennis, this is Beryl, she was just leaving," Merle stammered.

"Hi Dennis, so pleased to meet you. No rush really Merle, I have time for one more drink and it's my shout," Beryl replied placing a fifty dollar note on the bar.

Merle looked in disbelief, never before having seen Beryl place so much money on the counter for drinks.

She was speechless when Beryl purred, "What do you do for a living Dennis?"

"Actually I work for a mining company and am down here for a meeting, I live in Brisbane," Dennis explained.

"What does your wife do while you're away Dennis?" Beryl asked looking at Merle who, by now, was smouldering.

"Well," said Dennis coughing self-consciously, "Anne plays golf and works for a few charities."

"Must go now, take care Dennis," Beryl replied finishing her drink and walking off to catch a cab home.

Beryl waved for a taxi, smiling at Merle as she arrived, panting.

"Ok Beryl, so what is your game? I am bloody furious, you did that on purpose. No mention was made that the man had to be single!" Merle fumed as the taxi pulled up and they both got in.

"Now Merle, what are you accusing me of? I was just being friendly!" Beryl smiled.

"Well I don't want you to be so fuckin' friendly the next time you see me with a man, just stay clear. Do you hear me?" Merle spat back as the cab arrived at the village. She jumped out slamming the door and walked off, shaking her head in fury.

Beryl felt good, she had two wins that night, the second and third in her life. Her confidence rose, she was more in control and it felt good to stand up to Merle who had really controlled her life for several years since she'd moved into the village. A battle was really on now.

Beryl showered and went to bed, planning to leave early in the morning so Merle would not be aware she had a date in the shopping centre with a man from out of town. Setting the alarm, now smugly confident, she swallowed two painkillers to ease not only a throbbing headache but also her arthritic pain before drifting off to sleep.

Sitting bolt upright in bed, grimacing with the pain in her head, Beryl was annoyed with herself for again drinking too much. Checking the time, she turned off the alarm clock deciding, although early she'd situate herself in the shopping complex ahead of time and watch for her date to turn up so she could check him out. If she thought him unsuitable she would feign illness and cancel the event despite him having flown in last night especially to meet her for lunch at midday.

Beryl had a good, healthy, hearty breakfast, high in energy to sustain her during the day, aware she may have to perform for the first time in two decades. Excited at the prospect she took a long shower, put on her new dress and after applying makeup, nodded at the result in the mirror.

Counting out three hundred dollars with which she would buy herself some new clothes she placed the money in her wallet and hid the balance. Peering through the window, Beryl saw all was quiet, that nothing stirred and so gingerly stepped out into the chilly morning air, then quickly walked towards the cab rank. Glancing back her heart stopped, Merle was locking her door, also about to leave. In a panic, and knowing Merle was too busy checking out her unit for signs of life to have seen her, Beryl jumped over the hedge in front of Bruce's unit, the only male resident in the complex. Beryl hurried to hide around the back and in doing so fell over a water hose, head first into a rose bush. Extracting herself, she glanced at her dress now in shreds and sitting there partially hidden she watched Merle go past before disappearing onto the street in front of the complex.

'Fuck!' Beryl sobbed. Pulling herself up onto the windowsill and unable to avoid looking into Bruce's unit, she gulped. There lay Bruce, the friendly old man she thought was only having cups of tea with the bevy of smiling old women who visited him, naked with one of the older ladies. Still unable to take her eyes off the scene, she stared at his penis, the biggest she had ever seen, laying contentedly over her next-door neighbour's arm.

Although stunned, Beryl staggered onto the street and made her way home to change, determined to keep her date. Her mind raced, this was a sex mad house, and thought, 'bloody randy old Bruce, no wonder he is always smiling.' Several times when she first arrived, he had invited her over for morning tea. Bloody hell, she laughed, 'had I visited he would be knocking me off too, the old bugger.' No wonder the female residents came out looking contented, they hadn't just been in for morning tea they'd been with him all bloody night shagging!

Quickly Beryl showered, lucky that none of the scratches were on her face and choosing a favourite pair of slacks once again dressed. She was still determined to keep her appointment but even more determined to have a chat with old Bruce baby when she arrived home. The thought made her forget her trauma and she considered the scratches she had endured were well worth the fall.

Arriving at the mall, Beryl made her way to the café where she had arranged to meet Harold, her date and as she cautiously approached her heart skipped a beat, for there he was seated with Merle. Immediately she fathomed he had made two appointments, one with Merle at 10 am and the other with her at midday.

Turning away, Beryl decided to spend her spare hour buying some new clothes and as she was passing a lingerie shop, stopped abruptly. To win this bet she needed to take extraordinary steps and resolved to set about seducing old Bruce. Stepping inside she picked out the skimpiest pants and bra set she had ever seen, lacy and sexy. Even squeezing into the outfit made her feel hot, wet and ready for action. Gazing at old Bruce and his weapon that morning really turned her on and she had now made up her mind to win the bet that evening, come hell or high water.

Beryl knew she was in the king position meeting the date second in line, she would stymie any work Merle had done. Beryl smiled as she tried on new slacks and a dress from Kmart, the bet had turned mild mannered Beryl into a sexually charged, raving schemer. Beryl, now carrying her shopping, strolled through the mall. Glancing to her right she saw a flash of Merle leaving and slipped into a shop nearby to avoid her then stood quietly watching her get into a cab. Beryl smiled, the game was on, and she just had to win!

Having made her way back to the café she saw Harold still sitting at the same table, sedately reading a newspaper. Upon introducing herself Beryl sat down opposite him and smilingly enquired, "How was the flight, Harold?"

"Fine thanks. I am only here for the day, getting the late flight out this afternoon," he replied.

"Oh," Beryl replied, purposely sounding disappointed, "I thought we might get to know each other a little better while you are here."

"To be honest and brief, my sex days are over, but I'm offering free board and lodgings for companionship and a house keeper. There's no use me making promises I can't keep", he explained.

"Thanks for being honest Harold," a deflated Beryl replied, "but I need a car with an engine, frankly, my fire has not gone out just yet."

"Funny thing," Harold replied, "I met another lady this morning who told me the same thing. You see, I planned to meet a few today while I'm here."

"Good luck with that then Harold. Actually I'm not much of a cook anyway and my housekeeping is lousy these days," Beryl replied, now fully focused on the memory of Bruce's old penis.

Beryl did however enjoy their lunch, more so because she knew Merle had hit a brick wall also. Harold was just a genuine lonely old man simply looking for a free housekeeper and no doubt some woman would take him up on his offer. She had to admit he was good company and they parted friends promising to keep in touch via email.

Catching a cab home, Beryl began scheming how to get Bruce into bed that very night. Her juices were up and she was unable to get her mind off his beautiful looking penis, she had to have it and soon.

As it turned out, she did not have to knock on his door. Bruce was cleaning up the mess in his rose garden. He looked up and smiled as he saw her approaching, "For the love of me, Beryl, I can't work out why some idiot would want to vandalise my roses."

Beryl coughed, "Nothing surprises me these days Bruce, look I am going home to make a coffee would you like to join me? I'm sure after all your hard work you'd need one."

"Gee thanks Beryl," Bruce accepted happily, "sure can use one, say ten minutes?"

Beryl was ecstatic, almost out of breath after running home. She unpacked her shopping and prepared the coffee and cakes ready for Bruce's arrival. Her adrenalin was up and, throwing caution to the wind raced to the bedroom to undress and put on her sheer lace panties and bra. She then reapplied some makeup to hide her scratches and was just finishing when the doorbell rang.

Opening the door a small way, she saw Bruce waiting, smiling, "Sorry Bruce, I am not properly dressed yet, but what the hell, come in any way," she purred.

Bruce stepped in and gulped, "I can leave until you dress if you like," he drooled.

"Why bother, you've seen me now Bruce," Beryl replied, moving past him to the sink. Supremely confident in her power as a seductress, she poured the stunned Bruce a coffee.

Bruce sat down and they made small talk for a few minutes then he looked at Beryl and said, "Beryl, let's be straight up with one another, do you want to fuck or is this just show?"

"To be honest Bruce, I am in need of a good fuck, let's go for it right now," Beryl responded and now fully sexually aroused stood up, dropping her panties.

"Just wait a minute Beryl, I'll trot home and get a Viagra, I need it to get a proper hard on," Bruce replied bolting out the door leaving Beryl standing there panting with lust. Bruce returned and closing the door, stripped off, Beryl swooned at his half-erect penis, 'so beautiful' she thought.

Dragging him to the bedroom, Beryl almost threw him onto the bed, her eyes glazed as she focused on his rising penis and straddling him, groaned as she impaled herself. Beryl was in heaven as she began to rise up and down and Bruce was like a cat coming out of a dairy. With her libido rising she suddenly her right leg cramped causing her to roll off in agony. Bruce immediately turned and sitting astride her began to massage her leg. Finally the cramp let go and Beryl like a wild tigress having watched his penis throbbing over her face grabbed it and sucking on it madly begged him to mount her. Bruce responded and parting her legs entered her, pumping furiously as Beryl bucked like a horse, meeting each thrust until the cramp hit again. This time Bruce grabbed some Deep Heat from the dressing table and massaged the leg until the cramp eased.

Once again Bruce parted Beryl's legs, this time guiding his penis into her as she lay over the side of the bed. Beryl felt him ejaculate deep within her swollen vagina and for the first time in decades she reached a mind-blowing orgasm. Bruce collapsed onto Beryl gasping for breath and Beryl felt as though her fanny was on fire! It was then Bruce realised that some of the Deep Heat had rubbed off onto his cock when he'd guided it into her. They both raced to the bathroom, Bruce washing his penis and Beryl douching her hot fanny.

Looking at each other in the nude, both burst into uncontrollable laughter, "Listen Beryl, how come you asked me over this afternoon with the idea of seducing me into a sex session, we've lived here for a few years now and you've shown no interest before?" Bruce asked.

"Well, Brucey baby, I found out you have been fucking half the village and I needed a root to win a bet," explained Beryl laughing. He too laughed when she told him all about her bet with Merle.

"Just one thing Beryl, how did you know I was having it off with a few of the ladies?" Bruce asked bewildered, positive that none of his lovers would tell.

Beryl confessed all, telling him about her fall into his roses and both seeing the funny side of things, laughed until their sides hurt.

"Now Bruce, as you obviously like a bit of fanny, how about you make my day and go over and give Merle a good ride but don't tell her you have had it off with me," Beryl giggled as she washed Bruce's penis, which she noticed was on the rise again.

"Really Beryl, she seems so arrogant and hard to approach," Bruce replied.

"Come on Bruce, tell me how did you manage to get

into the pants of the other women?" Beryl asked.

"To be frank, it started when a couple of them talked about sex and I came straight to the point and asked, like I did with you, but there are only three of them Beryl, not the whole village. Strange, I think they are all aware of each other but choose not to discuss it and come over for the night when they feel like, it every couple of weeks or so," Bruce replied, adding "I know they enjoy it and the variety gives me a high. I think it would be hard now to settle for just one woman."

"I'm so sure our Merle is determined enough to win the bet and beat me that she would come across in a flash. It'd make my day to see the look on her face when she told me of her conquest, only to be told that you'd had me first," Beryl chuckled. Her naughty streak had surfaced after the good sex session and she felt young again, even wicked.

Bruce took up the challenge to seduce Merle. Beryl knew he liked his position in the village and to bed another resident would make his day. She watched as he knocked on Merle's door, sure the thought of fresh pussy would have him ready for action and watched as Merle smiled and looking both ways opened the door to let Bruce in.

Beryl showered, the rough sex had made her sore and the Deep Heat still stung her vagina. Wrapped in a dressing gown she sat watching the evening news and waited.

Chapter Three

At 9 pm she was so tired she decided to go to bed, it had been a long day. Falling into bed, she imagined Merle and Bruce going for it across the road, Merle thinking of her victory and gloating when she came over in the morning to claim her winnings.

Beryl knew she may have a few flings with Bruce, but that was about all. Old Bruce had a choice of lovers, he had the weapon and staying ability to satisfy women and he was in excellent health. No way was the cunning old bugger committing to any one of his lovers, he was in stud heaven and at his age had not much, if any, competition. She knew too that now hooked on the excitement she would pursue her interest in the dating site and see what happened. Each day she found opening her mail a real rush but, remembering Jean's warning to be aware of scammers looking for vulnerable women with money, she promised herself to remain cautious.

Waking to a knock on her door, she pulled on her dressing gown knowing who it would be and sure enough, opening the door there stood a smiling Merle, "Just came over Beryl to claim my winnings," she said with her hand out.

"Come in, who was the lucky man then?" Beryl said stepping aside for Merle to float in.

"You will never guess Beryl, not in a thousand years. It was Bruce from down the road. He must have been getting up the courage to ask for some time, poor dear, but he came over yesterday afternoon. Beryl, what a man, no kidding, best sex in my entire life, Bruce is a real bull," Merle crooned.

"Well done Merle. Just one thing wrong! Old Bruce had me first, gave me a real work over and he is fucking three others in the village on a regular basis," Beryl announced to a stunned Merle.

"No bloody wonder the old prick took ages to come, he'd already served you. Did you send him over to me by any chance?" she asked.

"As a matter of fact, yes. I was too sore to accommodate him again so I told him you were horny and wanted a good hump. I agree with you Merle that his ability is above average but you owe me the money, as I won the bet," Beryl gloated.

"Yes I agree, you win Beryl. I can't say you cheated but it was a bit unfair setting me up like that. I will admit though it was nice to have sex again and I did enjoy the thrill and fun of the competition, so how about, 'double or nothing'? Except this time, let's be totally fair. It has to be someone outside the village that we don't already know," Merle suggested.

Beryl thought for a few seconds and replied, "Okay Merle, you're on, but let's not spoil our friendship, after all we have been mates for some time. You're right, it was exciting and old Bruce will want seconds from us both now, so at least we have a lover, albeit a shared one. Strange how the other lovers act as if nothing is going on, just shows that there are women who want sex in later life or at least a proportion of us do."

"You know Beryl, I tried all manner of tricks to outdo you, I was enjoying living for the first time in years and it was exciting, I felt young and wild again. I tell you what, last night was quality sex, Bruce left me well and truly satisfied, actually my fanny felt really warm afterwards," Merle explained.

Beryl told her about the Deep Heat and cramp and they fell about laughing as Beryl made morning tea. The ice was broken and any bad feelings evaporated. They agreed to share their experiences on the dating site and whoever wins, so be it, the friendship would remain.

Both vowed to share any emails they received and act as backup on the first dates, just in case things did not go as planned. Instead of acting individually, they would now hunt as a pair deciding that it would be far more exciting to share the excitement.

The next message Beryl received was from a local and they agreed to meet up after only a week of chatting. His last few emails became a little saucy and Bernard promised to give Beryl a fine time in bed, even telling her what positions he liked best and asking her to do likewise. Beryl had learnt about the jockey style and a doggy from Jean and told Bernard she liked doggy, figuring cramp was less likely in that position.

Merle was not having much luck. Most prospects seemed like scammers after money and when another described in sick detail what he wanted to do to her she blocked him from her site.

Accompanying Beryl to the café where she was to meet Bernard, Merle watched from a distance as they met. He was a tall, good-looking man and all seemed fine as they sat down. The pair chatted for a couple of hours until both turned the subject to sex with Bernard finally asking Beryl if she felt like going somewhere to cement the relationship. Beryl was more than ready, she was now fully aroused and all common sense flew out the window. Since Bernard lived so far away she decided, against her better judgment, to let him drive them to her place.

Arriving back at her unit they slipped inside. Kissing passionately, Bernard lifted Beryl's skirt and fingered her, arousing her even more. Having guided him to her bedroom she shed her clothes and positioned herself doggy style as planned. Bernard stripped off and stood trying to get an erection while Beryl wet with anticipation watched the show in total frustration. Poor old Bernard had the smallest, most shrivelled dick she had ever seen. Even a good head job failed to raise Bernard, who flogged his tiny penis trying to get some action going.

"Sorry," he said, finally admitting, "it's been a few years since my wife died and this is the second time I've tried to get it up, even bloody Viagra doesn't help."

Now over it, the moment gone, Beryl began to dress, "Don't worry Bernard, it was nice meeting you anyway."

Poor old Bernard dressed and left. After all his emails promising Beryl a fucking good time, she felt a little deflated. She waved as he drove off and was about to close the door when she noticed old Bruce making his way up the road, so she stood holding the door open ready to have chat. Upon telling him of her disappointing tryst, Bruce's immediate response, as he was dropping his trousers exposing an already erect penis, was "Then, old girl, down on the carpet doggy style, it's Sheryl's night but she is crook and I've already taken a Viagra, so get set for a good rogering."

Beryl again undressed and knowing this time Bruce was more than ready she went down on all fours as instructed. He crouched over her, entering in one mighty thrust and she gasped for breath. True to his form, she became turned on by the slapping of his balls as he pounded her arse. A squishing sound as she became soaking wet made it more erotic and feeling an orgasm coming on she begged Bruce to push harder. Beryl was fully turned on and watched in awe as his face dripped sweat and his look changed to ecstasy as she felt him coming inside her. Finally they lay flat on the floor both panting, as he slipped from her.

"Bloody hell Beryl, that was amazing," Bruce marvelled, still breathing heavily.

"I have to confess Bruce that was the best, prolonged sex I have had in my life, you are amazing," Beryl panted.

"Come on let's get into bed," Bruce said as he helped her to her feet. Pulling the sheets back, Beryl felt unlike she had ever felt in her life before. 'If it had not been for Jean and Henry and the late night drinking session,' she thought, 'none of this would have ever happened.' Now locked in an embrace in bed with Bruce she felt empowered, even truly wanted and on a sexual high, her long suppressed feelings surfacing as she kissed him passionately this time. Wrapping her legs around him, the bed soaked beneath them from their sexual exploits, she felt Bruce pushing into her slowly and then they were joined as one, locked in an erotic embrace. Finally after what seemed like hours she felt his body shudder and they rolled apart, holding hands in the afterglow and both dozed off.

Beryl woke to find Bruce dressing and seeing she had awoken he bent over her giving her a big kiss, "Beryl, to be honest, I always fancied you, now I know why," he said, smiling.

"Come on Bruce, you have a harem of oldies panting for your services and I don't blame them," Beryl jested.

"Look Beryl, we sometimes get ourselves into situations we are not proud of, caused perhaps by vanity or lust. I have to go away for two weeks but I must tell you, of all, you are the best, the most passionate, sexual lady I have known," Bruce replied as he left, closing the front door behind him.

Beryl lay in bed, somehow sorry he had left, he had awakened feelings so long suppressed, never had she had such long satisfying sex. Confused she rolled over and dozed off again but woke to a knock on the door. Still naked but knowing it would be Merle wanting to go shopping she pulled on her dressing gown and answered the door.

"Come on in Merle, slept in a bit today, felt tired," Beryl yawned.

"Don't give me that Beryl, I saw Bruce leaving early, did he stay the night?" Merle quizzed.

"Look Merle, perhaps we should stop this silly dating thing and act our age," Beryl replied as she began making some coffee.

"Own up Beryl, you are in love with the old stud Bruce," Merle smirked.

"To a certain extent I really am, to be honest. He has awakened feelings in me I never knew existed Merle, he is a superb lover. I felt last night an intimacy and satisfaction I've never before experienced. Sadly though I am wise enough to know, apart from casual encounters, he is not about to give up his smorgasbord of fannies for me," Beryl replied casually, staring as if into space.

"I suppose you are right, in fact I am sorry it was not me he spent the night with. Did you know he was an airline pilot and although he was married once, has no family?" Merle informed her.

"Really, no I didn't. I guess then he's always had plenty of women at his beck and call. To be frank, I don't blame them, he is fantastic in bed …… and on the floor," Beryl giggled.

"Right, now get dressed, I have a date at the shopping centre so need my backup. Just remember that sometimes we cannot always have what we want," Merle replied.

"You are right Merle, no use staying home moping about, I have done plenty of that in my life. Strangely I am just becoming aware of how boring and miserable a life we lead here," Beryl said.

"I do agree that this whole episode has certainly got our juices flowing again and we can only hope all turns out well. At least we have bugger all to lose," Merle replied wistfully.

Chapter Four

Arriving at the shopping centre they noticed a scruffy looking man seated at a table reading a newspaper.

"Is that him?" Beryl asked.

"Maybe, he did have longish hair," Merle replied, "let's both go and see if it is him, he certainly doesn't look promising."

"Hi, are you Angus?" Merle asked.

"Yep ladies," Angus replied, "sit down, do yous wanna coffee?"

"Yes thanks," Merle replied, detecting a strong smell of body odour.

When Angus left to buy the coffees Beryl looked at Merle saying, "That man stinks like a sewer, I would say he hasn't had a bath for years."

"I agree, I sensed that first up and his bloody false teeth look green. He has to be the dirtiest prick I have seen in my life," Merle stood up as Angus returned with the coffees.

"Sorry Angus we have just had a phone call, my sister is sick and unfortunately we have to run," Merle told him as his odour became overbearing.

"If ya tell me your address then Merle I can drop round like, true what ya's say, we all need sex. I can do ya's both if ya like?" Angus grinned baring his green teeth.

"Nah, ya don't wanna root us Angus, we have the pox, an like, you need younger women, bein so good lookin' an all," Beryl said as they turned to leave.

Both scurried off leaving Angus looking perplexed. It seemed to him that all the women he met had some sort of urgent incident to attend to and that even the passing shoppers gave him a wide berth. 'Waste not, want not,' thought Angus as he poured a flask of brandy into one of the cups of coffee, 'back to the shelter and keep looking for a bed and some lonely old woman.'

"For fuck's sake Merle, be more careful next time, I can still smell his pong!" Beryl said as they both started to laugh.

"Stop it Beryl, I'm wetting my bloody pants," pleaded Merle, with tears streaming down her face.

"Come on, and for heaven's sake put your glasses on next time you look at their photos! Good job I have a date at Bingo this Thursday. Let's hope our luck changes," Beryl said, regaining her composure.

"You never told me that," Merle replied, frowning.

"I only made up my mind a few days ago. He's a good-looker and tells me he can go all night, but they all say that anyhow. Come on, my shout for lunch," Beryl offered.

Having enjoyed their lunch, Beryl bought Merle a new top, on sale at one of the clothing shops. Somehow, now Beryl found the whole thing tiring, she was quite prepared to share Bruce if she had to, after all one night of passion with him, she concluded, would be better than years of nothing. Their lovemaking had given her a new and broader perspective on life. Nothing compared to the fire he lit within her and her feeling of completeness when they were together. Other men, now especially after the Angus incident, seemed to offer little attraction.

Even the usual Thursday night ritual now seemed dull to Beryl. She'd had a taste of romance, 'no not romance', she thought, 'hot mind-blowing romance, with a man who was skilled in pleasing a woman.' With Jean and Henry still away they sat on their own enjoying the ritual drink watching the others file in, including Beryl's online date Richard, who even Merle agreed was one good-looker.

Introductions were made all round as Richard sat himself down and happily chatted to them both. He was very personable, well-dressed and clean cut but Beryl didn't seem too enthused.

When he left the table to buy a round of drinks Merle challenged her, "Look you seem a bit aloof Beryl, if you're not interested, I am."

"Okay, for some reason he doesn't light my fire Merle, by all means have a go, I will even help," Beryl replied.

The caller started the game as Richard returned with the drinks and although he did not seem too keen, he participated. Beryl played quietly while Merle came onto Richard who responded, aware his date was not that interested. Beryl smiled as Merle leaned forward at every opportunity displaying her breasts and it was quite obvious to Richard that he was on a winner.

Merle, now on fire, moved her chair closer to Richard and Beryl noticed his hand sliding up her dress. Merle parted her legs enough to allow his roving fingers to play with her.

What happened next even Beryl was unable to fully explain. A handbag was hurled over her head hitting a startled Richard, nearly knocking him off his seat.

"Caught you Richard, you bastard!" a woman screamed, "you and your fucking business trips, you piece of shit!"

Merle jumped up off the seat in shock, only to be knocked flat on the floor by a flying haymaker from the screaming, out of control female who then launched herself at poor old Richard. Beryl couldn't help but notice the look of fear on his face and several deep scratches oozing blood from his once perfect features.

Acting out of self-preservation, Beryl instinctively hauled Merle to her feet and beat a hasty exit from the venue, wondering if they would ever be welcome to return due to the embarrassment caused.

Engaging a waiting taxi, Beryl ordered the cabbie to drive home post-haste and neither spoke until safely ensconced in Beryl's unit. Both still in shock, Beryl guided Merle to the couch and poured two large whiskeys.

"What the hell happened?" Merle squeaked, now almost hysterical.

"I think the wife may have turned up Merle. Possibly just in time actually, or she'd have caught you two screwing under the table," Beryl replied, gulping down her drink.

"He was your date Beryl and I copped the flogging," Merle snivelled. "It was your fanny he had his arm up Merle, so one could assume it was you he was going to bang not me," Beryl argued, still trying to comprehend how she would ever be able to show her face at Bingo again.

"Shit, Beryl, I was not far off an orgasm, then the next thing I know I was on the floor. It was so erotic! I was miles away, hell, what a fool I must have looked," Merle whimpered.

"Who really cares Merle? It'll give all the old biddies something to gossip about for weeks. It was funny really, what a hoot, and I was about to yell 'Bingo' too! Can't blame the tigress though I suppose, she was only protecting her territory, the lying prick, although it goes on all the time," Beryl said, now laughing at the absurdity of it all.

"Fuck this online dating shit Beryl. At our age, any older, decent man is taken and we are the minority. I heard that there are seven older single women over sixty-five to each man, we have no chance," Merle declared, seeming defeated.

"No Merle. Now that we've stuffed up at Bingo, although I admit I was sick of it anyway, let's continue with our challenge, but just be more careful in future. Bruce proves there are some good men out there, so let's see what we can find.

What say we change our profiles! How about one of us is a 'hottie' looking for sex and the other is the 'no sex until marriage' type looking for a husband, then see what happens?" Beryl suggested.

"You can be the sexy one Beryl, I am going to be more discreet and even shrewd so let's make the husband seeker sound wealthy. Then I agree, it would be a challenge and an experiment also" said Merle, now calming after three strong drinks.

"Okay, off to bed we go then. Come over first thing tomorrow and we'll set up new profiles. Let's have some fun, bugger bingo!" Beryl remarked, ushering Merle out the door.

As planned, the following morning they both changed their profiles. Beryl made it quite clear that she was looking for a casual, but sexual, relationship. Merle put up a recent photo stating she was a widow of some wealth, looking for a future husband to travel with and to share her home.

Within three hours Merle had several responses. Some were from young men and some from gents overseas, many declaring they had fallen in love with her photo and promising undying love. Together they began to cultivate them and within days had received numerous heart breaking stories asking for various amounts of money in order for them to fly to Australia or from interstate, to meet their 'one true love'.

Strangely, Beryl only had a few replies. One older man seemed genuine so they arranged to meet him at the usual café in the shopping centre. Now, without bingo, this became a game and viewing it as a pastime, occupied their time.

Sitting in the café watching the passing parade, both commented on the large number of older people, especially couples and women who went by. Finally the date, Ian Fleming, arrived and after quick introductions sat down in a flourish and they all started to chat.

"What do you do Ian?" Beryl enquired.

"Actually can't say. It's top secret," Ian replied glancing about.

"Wow, must be exciting Ian," Merle replied, casting a look at Beryl who was trying to hide a smile.

'We have one here', thought Beryl, "Do you think it's

safe here for us Ian?" she asked, now trying hard not to laugh.

"It's just that they know where I am at all times Beryl, so better to be alert," Ian replied, glancing around suspiciously.

"Have you been looking long for love Ian?" Merle asked trying to sound genuine.

"Actually, my real name is James Bond and I have many affairs with agents from other countries, you are both delegates I can tell," Ian replied jumping up wild-eyed and running off.

Merle looked at Beryl and finally broke into laughter, "That was insane, and you reckon I can pick them Beryl, can you believe that?"

"I think we have led too sedate a life Merle. That was unreal. Sad really, he was well-dressed and good-looking but quite weird and obviously mentally unstable. Such a shame," Beryl replied, shaking her head.

With James Bond fleeing the scene, they decided to finish their coffee and spend some time shopping or browsing to fill in some of the afternoon. Both agreed that since the Jean and Henry late night dinner, life had become a little more exciting and by comparison, sitting at home watching the 'soapies' and cooking and gardening shows was so bloody boring it was now downright depressing. They wanted something different in their lives but, being so financially constrained, their options were somewhat limited.

Having sat longer than usual they were surprised when a tall, well- dressed man asked if he may join them as all the other tables were full. They agreed immediately and he placed his tray on the table and sat down.

"David Bond, pleased to meet you both and thanks for sharing the table," David greeted them.

"No relation to James I hope?" Merle replied, laughing. Seeing David looking perplexed Beryl told him their story, after which they all had a good laugh.

"I assure you girls that the same can occur with the female species. I tried the internet dating and met a few real weirdos, so gave up," David remarked.

Merle then told him of their meetings so far and the trio chatted and laughed for over an hour as the midday rush disappeared. David told them of one lady he met who was into tarot cards and the afterlife. They had only met twice when she wanted to exchange blood in some weird ceremony and had stalked him for some time. Thankfully, he told them, she only had his email address and in the end he had to change it.

"So far, we haven't had to go to that extreme David but after our experiences, nothing would surprise us," Beryl told him.

As they left David promised to join them at the club on Thursday. It seemed strange, but he only lived two blocks away from them. He gave them both a hug as they parted and as he left they agreed he seemed a nice normal man, but on past performance Merle, who was the keenest, declared 'steady as she goes'! On the way home Beryl questioned Merle, "Thought we weren't going back to the club Merle, after our last visit we may not be welcome?"

"Who cares? Since we started this mad bet Beryl,

somehow my life has changed and for the better. There we were waiting to die, bored shitless, now I am at least happy to be alive! I don't think I have ever laughed so much in my life and I tell you what, I have to admit Bruce reignited my fire too, he awoke feelings in me that I had suppressed for years! Do I care what the old biddies think? Shit no! We'll walk in, heads held high Beryl, fuck 'em!"

"I'm with you Merle, I agree we have both changed. I think we are daring to live the dream! Take a look at the other three girls in the village sneaking in to Bruce for a root, especially bloody Ethel, always gossiping about others. If it wasn't for old Bruce, I would soon spill the beans on her and her high and mighty ways," responded Beryl.

They returned home on a high, it had been an interesting day. Beryl made a light dinner as Merle checked their emails for any contacts and snacking on tuna and crackers, they discussed the mail.

Merle had one good prospect who stated he too was reasonably well off and so certainly would pay his own way if things worked out. All the others were blatantly obvious schemers, trying to con what they perceived to be a lonely, wealthy woman. Some of the rhetoric was so smooth they both laughed aloud but at the same time were saddened that some might be taken in by the schmaltz, no doubt written by experts in seducing lonely women.

Merle arranged to meet her admirer on Tuesday. He had suggested they meet at a local motel but she refused, saying she wished to meet on the first occasion at the shopping centre and that she would have a female friend with her.

On the arranged day, as they approached the café tables in the mall, Merle gave out a low whistle, "His name is Peter Dawes and if looks are anything to go by, I may be on a winner," Merle whispered excitedly.

Peter rose as they approached, pulling chairs out and seating them both. "Thanks for coming Merle and Beryl," he greeted them, "I must say Merle, you look even better in the flesh than in your photo!"

Merle blushed, "Thanks Peter, nice to meet you too, do you live nearby?"

"No, actually, I live on the North Shore and have a home there, but am on my own and it is a bit lonely," Peter replied.

Beryl, seeing they were obviously enjoying one another's company, decided to leave them to it and caught a cab home. As she was dropped off, her heart skipped a beat, Bruce's car was in the carport. He was home.

Unpacking her groceries quickly, she showered in case Bruce came over. Just as she was about to undress, a knock came on the door and her wish had been answered, Bruce stood there, smiling.

"Come on in Bruce, I was just about to shower, but no problems," Beryl greeted him.

"I just arrived home and saw the taxi drop you off. To be honest, I missed you while I was away and so came straight over. Since we both need a shower, shall we save water?" Bruce giggled enquiringly.

'Does a duck swim?' thought Beryl, as they began stripping off their clothes on the way to the shower.

Beryl didn't make it though as Bruce pulled her into the bedroom. Pushing her onto the bed Bruce moved her legs back under his arms, exposing her inviting vagina. What followed was a wild pounding of bodies and their pent up sexual frustration climaxing in a few short minutes.

Showering, they embraced under the water erotically kissing and gently washing each other, basking in the intimate touching.

Retiring to the bedroom, they fell into each other's arms, neither leaving the bed until the following morning, both on a high after a long night of passion.

Chapter Five

Enjoying breakfast, now comfortable in each other's presence, Beryl not only enjoyed the fantastic sex but the company Bruce provided, 'a happy chappie', she thought, 'he sure seems to enjoy life'.

"Beryl," he asked, "would you like to come down the coast with me next week? I have about five or six days to finish a project I am working on and the break might do you good."

"Do you mean that Bruce, have you a place to stay if I come?" Beryl replied, excited. This would be the first time she had a night away since she moved into her unit. Her heart was beating fast and she beamed at the thought of being asked to go on a romantic getaway.

"If you are going to the club Thursday, can I come as your date and to protect you?" Bruce laughed.

"Of course Bruce, I would love to have you escort me, what a thrill!" Beryl exclaimed.

"One thing though, perhaps it is going to be hard to keep me out of your bed now Beryl," Bruce replied.

"Didn't think I was that good in bed," Beryl said glowing with happiness.

"To be honest Beryl, you are one horny chick. I've never had anyone as good as you, you're completely relaxed and enjoy your sexuality. I find you exciting and just can't get enough of you," Bruce explained.

"You have no idea how you have boosted my ego Bruce,

my husband called me useless for so long that I believed it," responded Beryl.

"More fool him, what work did he do?" Bruce queried.

"He was a self-righteous union thug, full of his own importance and shagged every moll who would let him," Beryl replied, the first time ever feeling comfortable enough to express her true feelings.

"Let's clean up the brekkie things then I'll get the car and we'll go into town. I need a few things at the hardware shop and I'll shout lunch in town," Bruce suggested.

"No, you go and get ready, I'll wash up, make the bed and then come down," she remarked, ushering him to the door.

Beryl sang happily as she washed the cups and plates, then leaving them to dry, made the bed. Glancing back at the bed before leaving, she stood reminiscing on the wonderful night of passion they'd enjoyed.

A knock came on the door as Beryl was picking up her handbag. It was Merle with a smile on her face from ear to ear.

"Just spoke to our boy Bruce. I think he may be your boy now Beryl, he told me of your upcoming trip away next week," Merle gushed.

"I'd love to think that Merle, how was yesterday, all okay?" Beryl asked.

"Bloody disaster Beryl, went back to his house, got in the sack and had sex. By the way, did you smell something at the café yesterday?" Merle asked.

"No, not really, come on, explain what you mean," requested Beryl.

"Well, we had sex, but he kept farting. It was such a turn off and when he told me he had uncontrolled flatulence, I asked him to take me home," Merle replied.

Beryl couldn't stop herself laughing and Merle blushing, followed suit but shot back, "It was no laughing matter Beryl! It was bloody awful. I am about over this dating bullshit and it looks like old Bruce has you tied up now."

"I'd love to think that I had him tied up too. I am trying not to become jealous, but can't help it. How can I change the rules Merle, I seduced him when it suited me?" Beryl replied, closing the door.

"Beryl, at our age let's live each day as it comes, at least we have learnt to put ourselves out there, be true to our feelings and enjoy what we can," Merle suggested as she walked off.

Bruce was waiting, seated on the front porch. He jumped up smiling, and held the car door open for Beryl. What Merle told her in parting was true, live each day, by putting herself out there. She was now with a man friend going shopping, not by bus or taxi, but driven for the first time in years. It felt good as they travelled along chatting, Bruce was excellent company and she knew she was falling in love, perhaps truly for the first time in her life.

Stopping at a hardware store Bruce took Beryl by the hand as he made his way along the aisles, "What exactly are we looking for?" Beryl asked.

"Sorry, I should have said. Paint, I have just finished outfitting my yacht and all I have left to do is paint the galley and master bedroom," Bruce replied casually.

Beryl stopped dead in her tracks, enquiring, "Do you mean to tell me you have a yacht and that's what we will be sleeping on next week?"

"Yep, it's been a long project but nearly finished, my dream is to sail Northern Australia. That's why I purchased the unit in the village, it's secure enough there for me to just come and go," Bruce explained.

"Good heavens Bruce, what else haven't you told me, not that I have any right to ask I suppose?" Beryl queried.

"Of course you have. As a matter of fact I was going to suggest that maybe you might like to come with me Beryl?" he responded.

Beryl again stopped in her tracks, her mind in turmoil, she had never envisaged such a scenario. Looking at Bruce, she knew she was smitten but something had to be said and as they sat down on a bench seat in the garden section she spoke from the heart, "Really Bruce, I know I have no right to change the rules now to suit myself and my own feelings, but I can't be true to myself as part of your harem. To be honest, I want a sexual relationship with you but I just don't feel comfortable sharing you. I am a hypocrite perhaps having seduced you for a bet after all. I enjoy our lovemaking more than you can imagine but I have to try and find my own man, one who wants only me, to share what life I have left."

Beryl knew what he offered was a dream she would never realise but this was no longer a game and her happiness and conscience would suffer if she weren't honest. A tear ran down Beryl's cheek as she concluded, "We can still be friends though, if you like!"

Bruce leant over and kissed her, "Since our first sexual liaison, apart from Merle, I have not had another woman and do not intend to. I have fallen in love with you Beryl. I know I will have to prove myself and I will be true to you if you will only give me a go. I suppose I got carried away with all the attention and am truly sorry if it now comes between us. I intended to tell you all this on the yacht and alone, not in some hardware store," Bruce explained, almost pleadingly.

"Do you really mean that Bruce? I love you too, funny I knew that after the first night," Beryl confessed.

"You are the one for me Beryl. Actually, to show you I am genuine, let's marry before we leave and head into the wild blue yonder together as man and wife," Bruce proposed.

Beryl broke down completely, collapsing into Bruce's strong arms and they held each other tightly. Her wildest dreams had come true.

"Come on old girl, people are looking at us, let's pick the colour for our yacht's passion room," Bruce coaxed lovingly.

Beryl wiped her eyes, her life had changed. She must now play her part as a partner and she had to pull her weight. Like two youngsters, they talked plans and picked out several tins of paint before finding a restaurant and celebrating their partnership, both deliriously happy.

On the way home Bruce insisted on stopping at a bottle shop and buying a few bottles of wine, he promised Beryl he would personally visit each of the village women he had sex with and inform them of their forthcoming marriage. The sooner he faced his responsibility, he told her, the better, to save any embarrassment. He suggested also that he move in with Beryl, sell his unit and buy a half share in hers, as having two would be a waste of money in upkeep. Beryl thought this a great idea as the extra money would make life easier for her and Bruce insisted he would pay all the outgoings, assuring her he was comfortably well off.

True to his word, while Beryl started dinner, Bruce visited the three women to tell them his news. All wished him good luck but he knew they now resented Beryl, for all three themselves would have loved to have won his heart and he knew too that their sexual liaisons had given them great satisfaction.

Merle came over while Bruce was on his mission and when Beryl blurted out the startling news Merle embraced her, "Just goes to prove Beryl, you will never, never know if you never, never go! Thank heavens for a few drinks, quite a few, really," Merle laughed.

"I hope Merle you find someone too. I am just so happy, my whole life has changed. It all seems so surreal. Hold the faith Merle, don't give up on your dream," Beryl advised.

"I suppose Beryl told you the news," Bruce said to Merle when he came back in.

"Sure did Bruce, I am so happy for you both, I have to admit I am jealous, you are some stud," Merle laughed as they opened a bottle of wine.

"A stud needs a good mare Merle and I am not letting this one go, ever," Bruce laughed as they clinked glasses.

"Hard to believe you two lived so close for so long and never got together before now," Merle remarked.

"Come on Merle, Bruce was always in bed with his harem, we were the only two who didn't know there lived a stud amongst us," Beryl laughed happily.

"Steady on, I wasn't here that much." Bruce chipped in, "I've been working on the yacht for three long years and Beryl is the only one I have ever asked to join me, so I wasn't that keen."

"Be honest Bruce, you liked the attention," Merle giggled.

"Yes I did, to be fair it was nice having it laid on. Once I started I got hooked on the variety but I'm perfectly happy to settle for the spunky lady I now have in my bed," Bruce confessed.

The trio enjoyed a meal and a few drinks then all three went to Bruce's and helped him move a few items to Beryl's. Merle suggested they finish the move in the morning as she knew from their touching and glances that the two lovers were keen to bed each other.

Chapter Six

The following day they finished moving Bruce in with Beryl, all amused by the inquisitive stares of the other neighbours. Having decided to sell his unit furnished, Bruce listed it that afternoon. They'd already planned to go down to the marina the next Saturday and so that evening decided to have dinner at the club. Merle phoned David Bond inviting him to join them, explaining Beryl had a date and perhaps he would care to make a foursome. He agreed enthusiastically.

Surprisingly no one took any notice of the two women as they entered the club with Bruce, seemingly the incident they had starred in was now forgotten. Once they were seated, Bruce went to the bar for drinks.

Beryl looked at Merle, "I have you to thank for all of this Merle, if it had not been for you making that crazy bet, none of this would have happened. I was just so bloody bored and miserable back then but now for some reason my aches and pains have disappeared, I truly am living the dream, all credit to you."

"I'm happy to take the credit and I do agree, that one mad, drunken bet has definitely changed our lives. I can tell you Beryl there's no going back for me either," Merle replied as she saw David making his way into the club. He smiled and gave her a little wave when he noticed her and joined them, sitting beside her at the table.

"First time here for years girls, you will have to teach

me this Bingo stuff," he laughed.

"To be honest David, I am over this Bingo shit myself. I'm all for getting myself a good partner like Beryl has and hopefully find more to do than play Bingo," Merle replied in her usually straight forward manner.

Bruce returned with the drinks, placing them on the table and shook hands with David, "Small world, how did you meet these two foxy chicks, what do you want to drink?" Bruce obviously had met David before.

"Just a beer thanks Bruce. Met the girls in town having coffee," David replied as Bruce headed back to the bar.

"Okay David, how do you know my Bruce?" Beryl quizzed.

"I was his solicitor until I retired," David answered.

Henry and Jean appeared and pulled up another two chairs. Jean sat down while Henry joined Bruce at the bar and ordered some drinks.

"Any news girls?" Jean asked.

"Yes Jean, Beryl is off the dating site for sure. She and Bruce now share her unit and she is off down the coast this week with him to finish off his yacht, ready to sail into the sunset," Merle informed her.

"Wow Beryl, that was quick! How about you Merle? David seems a nice person," Jean replied, batting her eyelids at David.

"We have just met Jean, I hope it may lead to more though," David replied on Merle's behalf.

Merle glanced at David unaware he had any real interest in her, but he now had her undivided attention and she smiled seductively at him. Beryl mused, 'you have no chance David old chap, Merle will have you in bed tonight, no problems.'

The game started and as usual Henry dutifully kept all glasses full, glad of the distraction as he found Bingo boring. During the evening, David and Bruce revived their old friendship and Bruce invited both he and Merle down to the yacht for a few days during the coming week.

On leaving the club, David offered to take Merle home. Waving them off, Beryl knew Merle would also be off the dating site the following morning. 'Although,' she mused, 'they had not met their new partners on a dating site, it had in fact been the catalyst for finding them.'

Arriving back at their now shared unit, Beryl noticed Merle had not returned. Bruce informed her that she had gone to David's house and no doubt if all went well, would probably not return to the village. He knew David was a lost and lonely person, having lived on his own now for several years.

As they undressed, Beryl watched Bruce hanging up his clothes. Smiling, she thought of how her late husband threw his clothes on the floor and fell into bed, usually drunk and smelling of cheap perfume. Now she had someone who looked after himself. Pulling back the sheets, they locked in an embrace and as he rolled onto her she felt his hardness press against her. Wrapping her legs around him, she gave a little sigh as he entered her and they lay as one.

Setting off on their trip to the yacht anchored at Bateman's Bay, Beryl revelled in the scenery as Bruce drove down the coast, too ashamed to admit she hadn't before left

Sydney in her entire life. The scenery of the several small villages they passed was breath-taking. David and Merle followed behind and as arranged they stopped at Kiama on the foreshore for lunch.

Beryl and Merle unpacked the lunch while Bruce and David checked out some of the yachts anchored at the jetty.

"Come on Merle, be honest, how are things going with David?" Beryl asked.

"Beryl, I hope I don't wake up to find this is just a dream. We spent the most magic two days at his house. David is no stud like old Bruce but he is a wonderfully kind man and he treats me like a princess," Merle replied.

"Has he told you of his intentions?" she enquired.

"No, not really, but he talks about what we are going to do. Don't tell Bruce, but if he asks, we're happy to come sailing with you. I have both fingers crossed that he will. Beryl if all this falls through, how can I ever go back to living like we used to? For me truthfully, now that you are going, I would pine away and die in misery," Merle declared with tears in her eyes.

"Come on cheer up, think positive, leave Bruce to me Merle. We started this crazy change of life thing together and we will finish it together," Beryl countered, hugging Merle.

The four enjoyed lunch as they watched the masts of the yachts swaying to and fro. Beryl knew Merle was absolutely right, to be part of this life, so foreign to what they had lived till now, was indeed dream-like. She again reflected on how none of this would have come to pass had it not been for her determination to win a stupid bet she made when drunk just to show Merle up. A bet she would never had made or even contemplated when sober. Now, although she felt rather ashamed of her behaviour, feelings she had never experienced before had been woken within her. Now too she had more self-confidence, no doubt due in part to her wonderfully satisfying love life with a partner she adored and those feelings she knew, were mutual.

Admittedly the whole affair with Bruce had been rather hasty but, at her age and stage in life, time was of the essence and she must now grab this opportunity to enjoy every hour and minute, living her dream.

On the drive down Bruce enquired of Beryl as to why she had never learnt to drive. She explained that her late husband simply wanted her to stay at home, raise the children and keep house. He considered a woman needed no further knowledge or skills and that included driving. He glanced across at her and smilingly replied, "Well Beryl, no reason for you not to learn now, we will get you a learner's permit first thing in the morning."

They arrived at Bateman's Bay at 3 pm having bought groceries and other supplies on the way.

Arriving at the marina hosting dozens of boats of all sizes and shapes, they strolled along the jetty single file behind Bruce until he stopped beside a large twenty-metre schooner sitting gracefully alongside.

"This is it folks," Bruce said, pointing to the magnificent looking vessel. Beryl gasped in awe, never envisaging he would have taken on a task to refurbish such a large yacht.

David and Merle climbed onto the deck whilst Beryl,

heart pounding, waited for Bruce to help her on board.

"Wow Bruce, how could you afford this?" Beryl gasped.

"Well now you know why I sold my house and all my other assets. I was mad really, but I too had a dream. It was nearly past resurrection when I purchased it," he laughed, and it's taken me three long years to get this far."

Bruce further explained that a friend of his owned the marina and had allowed him a cheap berth. Otherwise, he told them, he would have been unable to afford the costs of sailing it to Sydney.

"You are my hero Bruce," David laughed with him, "I'm impressed. I wish I'd had the guts to do something like this!"

"So now you know why I am selling my unit and buying half of Beryl's," Bruce explained, "we need the cash to fund our expedition and if we sink her and survive we'll end up back at the village playing Bingo."

"Like hell we will Bruce! We have my funds as well, we're partners in this crazy venture," Beryl proclaimed as she charged about the boat checking everything out.

Bruce guided them to the master bedroom, complete with walk in robes, far different from what she had imagined. On the bed Beryl noticed, was a double sleeping bag and glanced questioningly at Bruce. "After we finish painting we'll buy proper bedding," responded a smiling Bruce.

"Can we have the room opposite?" asked David.

"Actually that would be best, it is the larger of the remaining rooms and close to the shower and toilet," Bruce replied.

"I have to tell you Bruce, what you have achieved is

totally amazing. Speaking for myself, and I hope for Merle, we'd love to come on your adventure and of course would pay our fair share," David said with a look of almost pleading on his face.

"Well, strange as it may seem, I was going to ask Beryl if she would like Merle along, so if Beryl agrees it's a deal," Bruce remarked.

"Of course I agree. To be honest, Merle and I talked about just that and I planned to ask you Bruce, if they might join us," responded Beryl.

"Okay then, all agreed. Let's unload the car and go for dinner at the pub down the road to celebrate. We can start painting in the morning and perhaps take her out for a sail on an overnight trip before we go home," replied a happy Bruce.

Merle was so overcome she blubbered, "Big boat, big dick," as she hugged Bruce.

David looked stunned.

"Oh fuck, sorry David," Merle replied, explaining to him what had happened between her and Bruce.

"It was my fault," admitted Beryl. "At that time we were actually only bonking Bruce because of the crazy bet and in order to win I set her up by sending Bruce over. I now feel a bit bad about the whole thing but it did inspire our romance and all this," she added, opening her arms wide to take in the scene of the four of them together in the cabin of the yacht.

Awaiting David's reaction to what he had been told, they were somewhat relieved when he began to smile. "Listen folks," he said, "we are all mature adults and it's actually quite a funny story, but it was before I started dating Merle, so none of my business. Let's get real and forget the whole thing, what is done is done and I have had a few bonking buddies as well, so who am I to judge? At our age we are lucky to still be sexually active, so let's enjoy."

"Great! Now that's out in the open we don't have to pretend to be prudes in each other's presence. It's good not to have to hide anything, especially in the tropics," Beryl declared.

Moving their gear from both vehicles to the yacht, the four friends soon forgot Merle's indiscretion and piling into David's vehicle drove to the pub for dinner.

As the women were sitting at the table waiting for the men to buy drinks and place the meal orders, Beryl could hardly contain her laughter, "Fuck Merle, I can't believe you said that!"

"Shit Beryl, I was so overcome with happiness it just came out! It is true though, old Bruce does have a big dick and he is a master shagger. David has about three pumps and blows. Once things settle down I am going to suggest to him that Viagra may help him last longer! You really are lucky Beryl. I now wish I hadn't fucked Bruce at all, he's set such a high bench mark," Merle replied.

"He is a lovely man though, your David. Just think, what a time we'll have," Beryl remarked.

"I know Beryl, we are both lucky and I'm glad we put ourselves out there. If we'd continued watching soapies and leading the boring shit lives we were, none of this would have happened. Like you, my aches and pains seem to have all gone," Merle replied as their men, both laughing, returned with drinks.

"Okay, what are you two laughing at?" Merle asked.

"Nothing really, just being dirty old men. We've agreed we've got a couple of spunky chicks now and we were gloating about how lucky we are," David replied, "and Merle, get ready tonight my girl, I've had a chat with Bruce and he's dishing me out a Viagra so I can sustain an erection!"

"I believe many things in life would be far better if people were to be more candid about themselves," Bruce said, "so David and I have decided to be open in expressing our true feelings. Since we'll be living together next month in a confined space, it will work better if we are all straightforward with each other," he added.

"Done! After all, our main objective has to be enjoying what life we have left, with no spin on things and no lies or any bullshit, unlike our politicians," Merle declared.

As best friends, the happy foursome left the hotel with a couple of bottles of wine and returned to the yacht. With the marina lights twinkling and the gentle lapping of the water against the moored craft, it was an intoxicating atmosphere. They enjoyed the wine and retired to bed at midnight, exhausted. It had been a long day.

Beryl woke at daylight and made her way cautiously to the toilet. All was quiet until she heard Merle groaning softly and the bed squeaking across the galley way. Smiling, she left her panties off and returned to a slumbering Bruce. He woke as soon as she began gently massaging his penis, and he too smiled. Beryl indicated to the next door and when he heard the lovemaking in progress he needed no more teasing. The sounds were erotic and like a raging bull, with one wild thrust he was into her. Beryl gasped as he rode her, pounding away like a mad man then groaned and collapsed on to her. "That was wild Beryl," Bruce panted, "but I'm the one who came early. Just listen, those buggers are still at it.

"A wild ride is sometimes all we need, lover. Let's get dressed and do some work," Beryl giggled.

They enjoyed a quick shower together and were eating breakfast when Merle came out looking bedraggled, but dressed. Pouring herself a coffee she looked at Bruce, "Thanks for the Viagra Bruce, David is off to a doctor today to get a prescription, hope I can last the distance," Merle laughed.

David joined them at the table, looking like a cat coming from the dairy, but dressed ready for work. No one spoke until they'd finished breakfast and had started the last of the restorations. The painting of the cabins. Excited that in a few days the old yacht would have her shakedown cruise, Merle and Beryl many times hugged each other in glee. A new era had begun for them both.

Chapter Seven

Now on a quest, all four set to work, sanding and preparing the last three cabins for painting. All that would then remain to be done was to fit them out with bedding. David and Merle agreed to furnish their cabin, to contribute half the cost of stocking the kitchen galley and when the truck arrived to fill the fuel tanks David insisted he pay half the fuel costs. This was by way of cementing the joint venture.

For three long days they toiled before standing back, totally satisfied with the final inspection of their work. David attended a doctor's appointment and Beryl proudly obtained a permit to learn to drive. Beryl, like the others, was glad Bruce had chosen Bateman's Bay to moor the yacht, all agreeing that being here was part of starting a new way of life.

By that evening the beds were made up properly with new bedding and the galley completely stocked with food and wine. It was then they decided to cook their first proper meal on board before setting sail the following morning for their shakedown day cruise.

Merle and Beryl like two excited teenagers, prepared dinner as they sipped on wine and chatted nonstop.

"David picked up the Viagra today Beryl, so it's 'look out tonight Merle old girl'!" Merle giggled. "The other night after Bruce gave him one, it took me an hour to get him down. I'm glad I've had three nights' rest," she added.

"Things have relaxed a bit with us too and I think it's better with a few nights between sessions! I was worried Bruce was going to bonk every night but he seems to have settled somewhat," Beryl advised.

"David wants to sell his house and move into the village with me. He thinks what you and Bruce have done is wise and I've agreed to sell him half my unit so I'll have some funds also. It'll make life easier," Merle happily informed Beryl.

"That's great news Merle, and Bruce had some too. His agent called him today confirming that his unit had been sold to a single lady. I can't believe how fast it happened. I wonder what she'll say when she finds out what went on in the master bedroom!" laughed Beryl.

"I suppose she'll act disgusted like most of the other old biddies, but your Bruce assured me they'd all be up for a good rogering if given half a chance! Just like the three I'd see leaving his unit on their respective appointed days, all looking contented," Merle replied.

"In truth Merle we were the same but now to be frank, for us to return to our miserable bloody lives would be an impossibility, so let's keep it up Merle. Better still, let's keep our men up and our knickers down," Beryl suggested as she sipped on another glass of wine.

"I'll drink to that Beryl. Gosh, can you believe how decadent we've become? I love it!" Merle declared, pouring herself another wine also.

After quick showers, Bruce and David joined them and the four enjoyed a wonderful meal, delighting in each other's company. Beryl knew Bruce was happy now that the three long years of work had ended and that his dream was coming to fruition. Pouring a wine, he patted her on the bum and as she turned, he kissed her gently. Gazing into his eyes she realised it was true love she felt for this man but best of all, she knew he loved her too.

Beryl noticed that Merle's sometimes caustic personality had gone. Perhaps it had been a form of defence and that deep down she had just been a lonely and insecure person. Now however as she gazed at David, she appeared happy and content, smiling at him each time their eyes met.

The women finished off the last bottle of wine as the men cleaned up the table and washed up, both happy with sharing such duties.

Beryl had an overwhelming urge to go to bed, she needed to be in the arms of her lover. As the last dish was stacked away she rose majestically and fuelled by alcohol she grabbed Bruce by the hand, leading him to their bedroom. Content to just wrap themselves in each other's arms, they were asleep in minutes, the toil of the past few days having taken their toll.

Waking with the feeling someone was present, she peered into the early morning light from the cabin porthole. She saw Merle's outline shuffling towards her. "Beryl, are you awake?" Merle whispered.

"Now I am, what's up?" Beryl asked.

"David forgot he'd taken a Viagra early in the night and took a second just before we went to bed. I am red raw, I can't pee without it hurting, bloody went for five hours trying to get him down, even he is getting worried!" Merle blurted out, sniffling.

Bruce now awake had overhead and said, "No problems, I'll phone the hospital. I've heard this happens occasionally so tell David not to worry," Bruce instructed as he pulled his trousers on.

David was sitting on a chair in the galley wrapped in his dressing gown, "Sorry for all this, I feel such a bloody fool, it just won't go down," reported David, looking sheepish.

"I think I need to see a doctor too, five hours of sex at my age has made me sore, great for the first hour but the longer I tried, the harder David became," Merle explained, still sniffling.

Arriving at the outpatients department, they were pleased to see there were only a few people waiting, due no doubt to the early hour. Bruce knew it would have been better for David to visit the doctor he had already seen, but making him wait until 9 am for his clinic to open seem too unkind.

He helped David shuffle to reception while Beryl comforted Merle. Both patients noticeably bent over and in pain. The male receptionist tried desperately to suppress a smile when informed of their problems.

A wheel-chair was found post-haste for David and he was taken for treatment to alleviate his problem. In the meantime an intern attended to Merle, applying soothing gel and antibiotic cream to her swollen and very sore vagina, with which she had bravely tried to pound David's stiffened appendage into submission.

Some two hours later the four were in the galley of the yacht sipping coffee not yet seeing the funny side of the horrendous morning they had all endured.

"I tell you what David, from now you can only have one Viagra a week and that will not be for a couple of weeks yet. My poor vagina has had six months' sex in one night and I smell like a brothel," Merle said so seriously that they all cracked up laughing.

"Come on, let's get back to reality. David can cast us off and we'll go for a sail, it'll take our minds off the dangers of Viagra," Bruce declared, still laughing.

Beryl stood alongside Merle as they cruised out of the marina into the bay. The sun was shining and the water flat and calm as they glided along. Bruce had been wise enough to install automatic machinery to raise and lower the sails without much human intervention, aware at the time that his crew may be of his own vintage and need all the modern sailing assistance available.

As they entered the headlands, the sails slowly unfurled for the first time, filling with the breeze. Beryl stood transfixed. All this was such a new and exciting experience. She felt euphoric, it was uplifting.

Bruce, his dreams now a reality, swept along down the coast in full sail. Even he was surprised at the speed with which the majestic old vessel virtually skimmed along over the ocean. However, he knew to be aware and prepared for much harsher conditions, for as careful as they may be in the future, being caught in inclement weather can happen at any time.

They tied up at the marina several hours later after having shared a wonderful experience. Several times Bruce had noticed Beryl on the bow of the vessel holding her arms out into the stiffening breeze then smiling back at him and blowing kisses like a wild, young teenager - a free spirit, released at last.

Later that evening, having returned to Sydney and their unit, Beryl made love like she had never done before, wild and without restraint, surprising even Bruce, her age of no consequence. To her, romance, love and life were meant to be enjoyed by all and not the domain of any age group. She knew now that only death would end her desire to enjoy the intimacy and warmth of loving Bruce and being loved by him in return.

Chapter Eight

Listening to him singing happily in the kitchen Beryl lay in bed waiting for her morning coffee.

Turning on the TV, as she had done on many lonely mornings in the past when she had time to fill in and no reason to get out of bed, she immediately turned it off again. She was no longer capable of watching the politicians, those who are supposed to govern in the best interests of the people, tell lies and utter bullshit. 'Why do they consider the average Australian so stupid?' she fumed. Throwing the remote control into the wastebasket by the bed, she vowed to at least live the balance of her life without listening to the crap they spewed.

Bruce returned, placing coffee and toast on her bedside table then went to retrieve his own breakfast and set it on his side. Jumping back into bed he looked at Beryl, "Last night Beryl, was the wildest sex I have had in my life, what caused that?" Bruce asked while munching on his toast, "Not that I'm complaining mind you!" he added.

"Well, to be honest, after the last few days on the yacht, I'd decided to let my feelings and actions run free. All my life I've been doing what others expected of me, not what I really wanted to do or to experience myself. Now that I'm in my twilight years I am going to catch up, so watch out Bruce, your Beryl is going to do everything to the maximum," was the candid reply.

"You know, that is exactly what I decided to do a few

years ago. I suppose that's why I wanted to experience as much sex as possible while I was still capable. So as far as I am concerned, let's go for it," Bruce exclaimed.

"I'm glad we have such an honest and open relationship. I intend experimenting with sex to satisfy you and to keep us wanting each other. I have heard the names of many different sexual acts but can only surmise what they mean," Beryl admitted.

"I tell you what, I have a couple of pornos packed in my bags. How about we watch one tonight and learn a few tricks!" Bruce suggested.

"Bloody hell, really Bruce? I've never seen one, bring it on! After dinner tonight let's shower and go for it. I'll do to you what they do," Beryl promised.

"Okay, done. David wants us to help him move into Merle's and clean his place up for sale. I told him we'd be there at ten," Bruce said, glancing at his watch.

"Great, let's go," Beryl said, getting out of bed still in the nude.

"Hurry up and put some clothes on Beryl or we'll end up being late," Bruce laughed.

"You are a sexy stud, aren't you? Save it for tonight, big boy," Beryl giggled.

Leaving the breakfast dishes in the sink due to time constraints, they headed over to David and Merle. Arriving just after the appointed hour, they found them both still in bed. Merle came to the door wiping sleep from her eyes, "Sorry guys, we slept in after all the work and then the trauma of David's permanent erection. We were both exhausted," Merle explained as she greeted them.

"Come on Merle, we know what you two were up to," Beryl laughed.

"No way. After the rogering I got Beryl, David can forget about sex for some time, nothing is further from my mind," Merle declared as she ushered them in.

Looking around the unit, Beryl considered it large and modern, well-furnished and spotlessly clean.

"Thanks for coming over," David greeted them, "I intend to sell it fully furnished. Second-hand stuff is hard to sell in our affluent society and Merle has her place furnished nicely so we'll just pack the personal items and a couple of my favourite paintings."

Beryl and Bruce filled their car with the boxes and cases already packed and Merle gave them her key to drop it off. She and David would continue with the packing while they were away and told them she figured with what they packed into David's car and another load in theirs, would finish the job. All the other odds and ends David would donate to charity.

As planned, after unloading the cartons and placing them inside Merle's unit, Beryl and Bruce returned to find David's car packed to almost overflowing!

"Surprising the junk one collects in his life, I suppose we are all guilty of it," David admitted.

"Sad part of life really but we all have to face reality and dispose of things we once thought important when we downgrade," Beryl remarked.

"Come on you lot, let's not get glum. I'll shout lunch at the club seeing it's only ten bucks a head today," Bruce offered, laughing.

Beryl nearly interjected to complain she would run herself short if they went out to lunch, but then it dawned on her that Bruce was paying. When the money for the share in her unit came through next month she would be able to indulge herself in such treats, previously unaffordable to her. She felt happy for Merle too. David was well cashed up and she would also have some independence when her sale was finalised. 'How their lives had taken a turn for the better,' she mused.

Entering the club, they were surprised to see Henry and Jean seated at a table, beckoning them over.

Henry asked Beryl what they had been up to, while Bruce and David as usual ordered lunch and bought drinks. Unable to control herself, she told them about their trip to the yacht and that David, having sustained a permanent erection had rogered Merle for hours.

Even Merle, now more relaxed than in the past, saw the funny side of things and they were all laughing heartily as David and Bruce returned with drinks.

"I suppose this pair of minxes have told you of my misfortune," David deduced.

"Bloody hell, Merle, are you all right?" Jean asked concerned.

"Let's put it this way Jean, I had enough sex in one long night to last me a year. My fault I suppose, I thought if I kept banging away 'it' would somehow collapse. Actually I became obsessed to succeed. I felt if I didn't, I'd have failed, not thinking it wasn't caused by me not performing well enough, but by the bloody Viagra," Merle confessed.

"Listen Bruce old chap, you are living my dream.

Overseas travel has become boring with the waiting for hours at airports, the cities busting with people and the bloody traffic. I long for some peace and tranquillity. You four are amazing people. I tell you what, if we can come along, I will fund all outgoings. To be honest I am no sailor, so money is all I can contribute," Henry offered, staring at Bruce and awaiting his answer.

Stunned a little by the offer, Bruce hesitated but after some thought replied, "I must admit Henry, six would be great as we need a nightly watch unless anchored. I agree but what about you other three? Bruce enquired of Beryl, Merle and David.

"I say okay, both helped me out when I needed it," Beryl replied.

"Merle, I promise to help with cooking and chores, so please, if Henry wants this I do too," Jean implored.

"I have no reason to say other than 'yes'. After all it is Bruce's boat and he says it would be best to have at least six on board. It is quite a large vessel and we do have an empty bedroom," Merle responded, with David nodding his head in agreement beside her.

"Just one thing Henry, I think it is unfair for you to pay all the costs. Considering Bruce paid for the yacht and has restored it, I want to share the costs with you," countered David.

"Fine David, I was more than happy to pay all costs but if that is what's agreed on, then so be it," Henry accepted.

"Done, we leave in three weeks for the Great Barrier Reef and beyond, with no time frame to return, so make your arrangements and welcome aboard," Bruce informed them as glasses were clinked by way of celebration.

It was quite late in the afternoon when they were ready to head home and so David suggested leaving the cars in the club car park as each of them would be over the limit if breathalysed. They needed no convincing given the pile of empties on the table and it was a happy bunch that stood waiting for taxis on the footpath.

Arriving at their unit, upon opening the door, Beryl chirped up, "Listen Bruce my boy, old Beryl is pissed! Can we leave the porno till tomorrow night? Neither of us would be capable of performing anyway. All I need now is bed, cuddles and sleep."

"Right as usual Beryl, you do look sexy, but old Bruce is as limp as a dead garden worm. Bed and sleep it is. I'll bring some water in, no doubt we'll need drinkies during the night. Bloody Henry, he was so happy about coming with us he just kept buying bottles of wine," slurred Bruce.

Falling into bed, they cuddled, rolled over and slipped into an alcohol induced sleep. Several times Beryl woke with a raging thirst and busting for a pee. On the third trip to the toilet she made a sacred oath never to over indulge in the evils of alcohol again. She had trouble balancing as she stood up but before she had time to pull her panties up, Bruce rushed past and vomited into the toilet bowl.

Slowly Beryl made her way to the bed, crashing onto the mattress. She felt really ill herself and could have done without the sight of Bruce throwing up.

Returning to bed, Bruce looked like death warmed up. Sitting with his head in his hands he looked like a sad old sheep dog who had just been admonished for some indiscretion, "Beryl, never let me drink like that again, a few is okay, but last night I think we all got carried away."

"I'm sure Henry thinks he has to keep large quantities of booze up to us. He seems to think it is his task in life to shout friends at the bar. Don't worry Bruce, this girl is off drinking sessions like that too, I'd far rather enjoy healthy bonking sessions, believe me. There is no contest between their afterglow and a hangover," Beryl declared, rubbing his back gently.

"True, neither of us is used to so much alcohol and it can't be good for us. Old Jean can put it away too so we'd better watch the bugger and restrict what he loads on the bloody yacht," Bruce replied as he lay on the bed staring at the ceiling, wondering why it was moving.

They slept until midday before slowly dressing and calling a cab to retrieve their car from the club car park. Returning home they knocked on the door of Merle's unit. Like them, both Merle and David had suffered a long painful night, promising never to indulge in any more such drinking sessions. Deciding instead to enjoy a bottle or two of wine on rare occasions.

Back in their own unit, Beryl made coffee, and still unable to face food they both returned to bed and slept most of the afternoon before finally rising and cooking a light meal for dinner.

"I hope you don't mind Beryl, but I want to put off the porno again. I must confess, the drinking session knocked me about quite a bit and it's no use you watching something if I can't quell your fire!" Bruce admitted, looking sheepish.

"Actually, I've been so ill I forgot about it. Tell you what, take me out for a driving lesson tomorrow. A nice drive up the coast will do us the world of good and then let's see how we feel," Beryl suggested and having settled on her suggestion, they undressed, kissed each other good night and slept soundly until morning.

Bruce had previously decided to save any possible arguments to pay a professional to teach Beryl to drive and at the appointed time, the instructor turned up. Immediately he realised, as Beryl pig-rooted and stalled the car, that he had made the right decision. Waving her and the poor instructor farewell, he watched them disappear before driving into the Registry Office to finalise the wedding plans he intended to surprise Beryl with. He would marry her on the yacht before departing on their trip.

Bruce decided to let Merle and Jean in on his plans and they readily agreed to help in the preparation, finding the whole affair exciting. He did wonder however if they would be capable of holding the secret they now shared, for a further two weeks.

Busy preparing lunch, Bruce heard a car pull up and looking out the window he saw Beryl, all smiles as the instructor drove off. Opening the door for her, a beaming Beryl chortled, "My instructor tells me, after a rough start, I am a natural."

"Glad to hear that my lovely. When you took off I feared it would take you some time to master the mechanics of driving," Bruce replied giving her a hug and patting her behind. "Let me tell you Bruce, I feel like doing something totally wild. How about after lunch we go to bed and watch your porno!" Beryl giggled.

"Funny, I felt a bit frisky too, my old lover, and took a Viagra while you were out. Let's forget lunch and go for it," Bruce suggested as they kissed passionately.

Beryl, now aware Bruce was more than ready for a wild session, happily made her way with him to the bedroom and they undressed, not taking their eyes off each other. She lay on the bed, legs apart, showing herself to Bruce while admiring his already erect penis. Placing the video in the player he fast-forwarded to the action. They teased each other in readiness for what was to come, fuelled by watching other couples having sex.

Never having seen such erotic behaviour, Beryl went down on Bruce giving him the first head job she had ever tried, taking her cue from the woman on screen.

The male actor then went down on his partner, as did Bruce. His tongue working in and out brought Beryl almost to orgasm and she begged Bruce to enter her. Unable to wait any longer, he slid up and over, entering her unguided. They locked lips in a deep kiss and, unable to control themselves any longer, reached orgasm together, even before the actors had begun coitus.

Lying together, they watched as the pair on screen had sex in many positions, before the woman finished off the session by again taking him in her mouth.

After the movie Beryl explained to Bruce, "I don't think I could do some of that or the anal bit, but admit it is a turn on watching a porno. This is the first time I've ever seen one and I must admit I'm still feeling sexual urges."

This time, Bruce slowly rose to the occasion and Beryl

sat on top, controlling a long and satisfying sexual union after which both were exhausted and dozed off.

Beryl woke with a start. Someone was knocking on the door. Wrapped in her dressing gown she answered to find Jean and Merle waiting, "Just came over see if you two want to come to the club for dinner," Merle smiled.

"Wait, I'll ask Bruce," Beryl replied.

"Gee, Beryl you smell like sex and we can tell you've been bonking," giggled Merle.

"Yes girls. To be honest, we watched a porno and shagged all afternoon," Beryl laughed as she turned and headed to the bedroom, returning quickly.

"Yep, Bruce is starving, we'll see you there," advised Beryl.

They showered together, both well and truly satisfied. All their sexual urges and feelings spent, the fire of passion quelled.

When Henry saw them enter the club both he and David headed to the bar area, "I'll go with the boys Beryl just to make sure we only have juice tonight, what do you reckon?" Bruce asked as she sat down.

"Yes for sure, I'm over alcohol for the time being," Beryl answered, smiling.

"Beryl tell us honestly, is a porno worth watching? Did it turn you on?" Merle fired, as soon as Bruce was out of earshot.

"Bloody hell, it sure was. What a turn on! We both went off!" Beryl giggled.

"Okay girls, let's get a few to take with us, we have to keep our sex lives interesting," Jean replied, eyes bright.

"I will send for some online in the morning. Actually I must admit, I've already looked at some sites on the internet," Merle replied as the men returned to the table, talking sailing.

"How is the driving going Beryl?" Merle asked.

"Great actually. I'm booking in for a test for my Licence before we leave and hopefully, fingers crossed, I'll get it," Beryl replied.

They spent the rest of the evening planning the trip. All more than a little excited about their forthcoming great adventure.

Chapter Nine

The following morning, as for the next few weeks, Beryl waited for her driving instructor, anxious to obtain her first Driver's Licence. Bruce smiled as he watched her drive off without incident. It was another big step in Beryl's new life. Even in the short time of their relationship he had seen her confidence and vitality grow.

Shaking his head, he wondered how he had overlooked her all these years. Although always friendly, he had never considered that underneath the façade laid a tigress whose sexual prowess, so long suppressed was just waiting for someone to uncover it.

Bruce chuckled to himself about 'life's little wonders' as he thought about the bet Beryl and Merle had between them. All the result of Henry providing them with copious quantities of alcohol in order to make himself popular.

The couples met twice weekly for dinner and as the wedding and departure date came ever closer, the excitement of the adventure, and unknown possibilities, grew daily. To Bruce it was a lifelong dream finally coming to fruition. He had often wondered who he'd invite to join him on his adventure and his relationship with Beryl had indeed solved that problem.

On the day before leaving for Bateman's Bay, they switched off the power to the fridge and ate out that night. Next morning they all met at the village and drove out in convoy, new horizons awaiting them. Word of their departure had spread, and as they left several of the village residents waved them farewell.

Two of Bruce's former lovers, forgetting their disappointment, came to wish them all the best. One announced that if she had an opportunity to seek some adventure in her twilight years she would take it in the blink of an eye. She even confessed to Beryl that she missed the sexual intimacy she had with Bruce and that it had made her feel young again. The other admitted she envied Beryl but held no hard feelings, she was simply grateful for the opportunity to have had one last fling.

Beryl couldn't fathom why Bruce and the others seemed to be in a hurry to get to the yacht, not stopping for morning tea as they had on the previous trip. Perhaps they were anxious to arrive early to buy the last minute items needed before departing the following morning on the tide.

As they pulled up, Beryl was surprised to see several people waiting patiently on the dock. She noticed a table in front of the yacht covered with a white cloth upon which sat a bouquet of yellow and white flowers, but still did not waking up to what was going on. Merle approached and said, with a broad grin on her face, "Come below Beryl, we have to dress the bride ready for her wedding. Hope you don't mind having Jean and me as your ladies in waiting."

Beryl stood stunned, looking at the bevy of smiling faces waiting for her reaction. Bruce, taking her in his arms and kissing her, whispered, "I told you we would be married before we left on our trip my love. The girls have worked hard to arrange all this."

"I'm speechless Bruce, I didn't give it another thought. In my life people have told me heaps but never kept their promises. I am honoured, you must truly love me," Beryl whispered back with tears running down her cheeks.

"Really truly, old thing! Now let's get this show on the road. I hope the dress fits okay," Bruce remarked as Merle and Jean, also caught up in the atmosphere and sniffling, guided Beryl to the bedroom and helped her dress in the lovely outfit they had so carefully chosen.

The wedding party soon arrived on deck looking resplendent and the guests gathered round to witness Bruce and Beryl become husband and wife. After the short ceremony, all retired to the local club to celebrate the wedding festivities. Beryl seemed overawed by the whole experience and let herself go completely, forgetting her oath not to imbibe alcohol. At midnight, the wedding party disbursed and Bruce guided his bride to the yacht where she collapsed on the bed, totally drunk. He helped her undress before sliding into bed next to her. Exhausted himself, he knew that the consummation of their marriage would have to wait!

Beryl woke with a start and looked at the time. Shaking a snoring Bruce she uttered, "Good heavens Bruce, it's 10 am. We'll never get away if we lay here all day!"

Bruce yawned as he replied, "We decided last night to stay over an extra day. We still have to unpack the vehicles and then some of our friends will drive them back to Sydney." "Great, oh 'husband of mine'. After yesterday I do need a day to recover," Beryl admitted, then rolling over and sitting on top of Bruce, suggesting that "perhaps now we should consummate the marriage!"

Beryl rubbed herself slowly up and down on Bruce and as his eyes glazed over she felt him harden to the teasing. The two were now locked in an erotic union, slowly becoming increasingly intensive. Beryl could tell from his eyes that he was coming and she felt him slowly slipping from her as he slumped forward.

Having showered and made coffee, Beryl noticed Henry and Jean unloading the last of the stores onto the yacht. "Morning guys, thanks for doing that, we slept in a bit," Beryl greeted them.

"Least we could do was to let the newlyweds have a lay in," Henry replied, "and David and Merle haven't surfaced yet anyway."

Beryl made a coffee for Bruce but found him still sleeping when she returned to the cabin so left the cup on his bedside table and wandered onto the bridge where she joined Jean, sitting in the sun and enjoying a coffee herself.

"Good morning Jean, where's Henry?" she asked.

"Oh dear Beryl, please keep this quiet. When we came home last night we decided to watch a porno. So here we are, sitting up in bed watching wide-eyed when I must have been overcome by alcohol or lust, and I grabbed poor Henry. I was giving him a head job when I bit too hard causing some damage and he's gone to the chemist to get some ointment to sooth his poor dick," whispered Jean, glancing around.

Beryl tried hard not to laugh as she enquired sympathetically "Heavens Jean, did it bleed?"

"No, but it was and still is a bit swollen. He still had sex with me though, he reckoned it was soothing and I must confess it felt good," Jean replied.

One by one the other crew members arose and Henry returned glancing at Jean, wondering if she had spilled the beans. He looked a bit sheepishly at the others and Beryl saw the relief on his face when no mention was made of Jean's passionate assault.

They waved the last of the guests away and too, those driving their vehicles back. Now as evening settled they were on their own, all retiring early to bed, on the eve of their big adventure.

Beryl woke the following morning to find Bruce missing from their bed, then realised the yacht was underway. Grabbing her dressing gown, she ran on deck, surprised to see full sails up and the land now far distant. Henry was with Bruce at the helm, chatting away, and giving Bruce a quick wave, she raced back to the cabin to dress.

All the hard work and planning was over and this was now very real, six 'grey nomads' living the dream. Each day a new adventure and all thanks to one man, her lover and now husband, Bruce. She smiled when she reflected on them living in the same retirement village for years, yet she had never known he was restoring a yacht, or, for that matter, that he was shagging several of the village ladies!

The others had already had breakfast and all seemed to be fitting in nicely with the daily routine they had planned. Jean and Merle packed the last of the stores and cleaned up the breakfast cups and plates. Bruce was teaching Henry about course plotting, while David checked out the rigging. As she ate her breakfast, Beryl watched all the on-board activity. 'Far better', she thought, 'than back in the village, always broke, watching stupid soaps and getting upset at politicians crapping on'.

Bruce decided to head to sea and to the Central Coast. No one had any inclination to sail into Sydney Heads as yet. Perhaps that would come later, at the end of this odyssey - whenever that may be.

On the second day out, Beryl suffered a little seasickness, as did Henry, but both recovered and eventually settled. Sailing into Swansea three days later and dropping anchor, they congratulated themselves on taking to their shipboard life so well. The sail up the coast had been breath-taking. Luckily a stiff breeze, and limited chop made the initial shakedown period reasonably comfortable, although sleeping with the vessel rolling took some adjustment.

As they had not used many of the stores, they decided to anchor overnight and sail off at daylight. No one seemed keen to hang about, they were all anxious to reach tropical waters as soon as possible. Bruce suggested heading out to sea and sailing to Queensland, admitting his wish had always been to sail the Whitsunday's and Northern Queensland, stopping at places like Cook Town and several of the Islands. All agreed it sounded romantic to swim in the waters and explore the many islands of Northern Australia.

Daylight the following morning saw the group again heading out to sea, the weather was again favourable and as they lost sight of land, several pods of dolphins skimmed along with them. Beryl noticed that no one had complained about aches and pains since the start of the journey and all fitted in agreeably together. Each couple took their responsibilities seriously and no one was ever late for their shift at the helm. Those off shift attended to odd jobs, prepared the meals and generally enjoyed the trip or rested in their cabins.

The days were getting warmer as they sailed north, finally anchoring at Broadwater on the Gold Coast. Here they restocked and visited some of the attractions. The women bought sarongs and bikinis, giggling and laughing as each tried on several sets, each skimpier than the one before. "Who cares what we look like girls," Jean chortled, "no one will see us on deck or on some remote Island."

Coming upon a hair and beauty salon, they all decided on new hairstyles and Brazilians. Beryl did not know what a Brazilian was until Jean explained it to her but nodded in agreement. This was all exciting and a new era for her.

Returning to the yacht after having dinner at one of the clubs, Beryl paraded in her new swimwear and flashed her smooth fanny at Bruce. Finding her quite irresistible, Bruce took advantage of the moment and the pair were soon wrapped in erotic lovemaking.

Anchoring in some cove or quiet bay each evening they began to slow down, finding and exploring isolated islands, sun baking and skinny dipping, cooking on the beach, scavenging for shells and other little mementos and generally having a ball. Their past lives completely forgotten.

Many evenings as they sat watching the sun go

down, enjoying a quiet drink and reflecting on their past lives, all agreed that life goes on, that one must never give up, that you must be prepared to put yourself out there and go for it. Love, lust and sexuality can be with you until death, you simply have to accept change and, just as in the book, *'Dare to Live the Dream'*.

The End

Lance C Wilson

A NOVEL THAT WILL INSPIRE

Foreword

I hope you enjoy *'Meg's Story'*. Like my initial two books, penned now what seems so long ago, it is loosely based on fact as told to me by someone who is now a very good friend. The graphic sexual detail of Indian practices may offend but in reality this story could not be told if they had not been included.

When passing an individual in the street it is perhaps true to say that, unbeknown to you, many have led extremely interesting lives. *'Meg's Story'* is one such story. Although I have used poetic license to highlight certain aspects, it remains one hell of a love story proving the fire of true passion extinguishes only on death.

Both my original novels, *'Dare to Live the Dream'* and *'Tears Over The Kimberleys'*, are based on stories I heard from or of outstanding and passionate individuals. Characters who dared to be different and whose lives were envied by those who never had the chance to do the things they'd often read or heard about.

'Meg's Story' is indeed uplifting and having spent time with the unique character I have based the story on, I am proud to present an account of her exceptional life. With her blessing, I have written this novel as fiction to protect those involved.

Some readers no doubt would have me apologise for the eroticism I've created in this novel, such as a lady reader who was so incensed by the sexual content of another of my novels that she phoned me one evening to scold me for including so much sex in the story. To my great amusement she went on to say she had stayed up until 3am that morning to finish reading the book and then asked if I had written any others as she would like to read them too! Need I say more?

Chapter One

The year is 1928. Perth in Western Australia is a quiet city, isolated from the rest of Australia by the tyranny of distance. On the opposite side of the Swan River looking towards Kings Park is a small leafy suburb and in a modest but comfortable house with a beautiful garden lived Peggy and Mark Jackson. Mark was a quiet, bespectacled public servant who had married Peggy simply because she was unable to find any other suitors. The cream of Australia's youth had been killed in the Great War a few years earlier, effectively causing a shortage of eligible bachelors.

Peggy Bresnehan was spoilt as a child by doting parents and, with the prospect of becoming an old maid, had pursued Mark Jackson merely because she saw an opportunity to gain a husband and some status in Perth's society. It had been her plan since meeting the eligible bachelor to push him into climbing the public service ladder to success. From day one the marriage had been a disaster. With his new wife always whining about something, the downtrodden Mark just let her rave on without response, frustrating the furious Peggy. Although they initially shared the same bed, Peggy just lay with legs apart showing no sexual interest in Mark while he relieved himself as quickly as possible. When, after only a year of marriage, Peggy became pregnant she quickly excused herself to the spare bedroom.

It was at this time that the hapless Mark simply

surrendered, fully aware he was doomed to be a servant of the overbearing Peggy and that any chance of him ever climbing the bureaucratic ladder disappeared into thin air, further frustrating the hopeful socialite.

Peggy became even more unbearable during the pregnancy, so every weekend Mark studiously worked in his garden. It was an escape and proved to be a window of happiness. Peggy meanwhile attended women's events and disregarded her husband, having accepted her plans seemed doomed and bitterly disappointed that her status in society would never reach her lofty expectations.

Perhaps the only small ray of happiness for Mark was the birth of his daughter, although Peggy completely ignored him as she lay regally in her hospital bed surrounded by her parents, friends and other relatives. As he looked upon the infant cradled in her mother's arms he knew his input into raising their child would be minimal. Despite being aware of this from day one, Mark became a devoted father. He had considered, before learning of the pregnancy, leaving his job and going interstate because his life had become such a misery, but on seeing his daughter all such thoughts never again entered his mind. He was content to dote on his daughter and satisfied himself with whatever time his wife allowed him to spend with her.

If Peggy had ignored her quiet unassuming husband before the birth of their daughter, it became far worse after she arrived. Peggy even breastfed in the confines of her bedroom and Mark meekly surrendered, reduced to the role of breadwinner.

One month after the birth, Margaret Maree Jackson was

christened in the Catholic Church, surrounded by family and friends. Both parents beamed with pride and no-one would have ever known there was friction between the couple. Peggy always showed a united family front in public for the sake of appearances and the affable Mark went along with it.

Peggy, now completely in charge of finances, set about saving frugally for Margaret's education, who to her disgust became known as 'Meg' to all, due to her besotted father calling her that, in the main just to piss Peggy off! Strangely enough though in time, with both parents doting on their only child, a strange relationship emerged. Peggy and Mark simply ignored each other while at the same time lived harmoniously with Meg as a family.

Even at a young age, with her beautiful blonde hair and striking facial features it soon became apparent Meg would be a beauty. It was apparent too that she was strong willed with a very feisty spirit. On weekends, Meg would play in the garden while her dad lovingly tended his flowers. Peggy would often try to intervene and return Meg to the confines of the house but on every occasion a great altercation would occur and as time passed Meg usually won. When she started school Meg proved to be a very bright child and popular with her classmates, soon becoming 'the leader of the pack'.

Peggy never returned to her husband's bed, not that she had yearnings for sexual contact with Mark, for in her dreams she envisioned rich and powerful men sweeping her off her feet and ravishing her. Many a night, although always with a sense of disgust at her weakness, her hands would wander beneath the sheets and her soft moans would drift across the confines of the bedroom.

To Peggy, Mark was simply a tool to avoid her becoming a spinster. She had never loved her husband, and in truth detested him, but appearances meant everything to Peggy and to seek sexual gratification outside the marriage was unthinkable.

As Meg grew, three events were to occur that would later have a great impact on her life. The first being that her mother became jealous of her as she matured early into a strikingly good-looking young woman.

In high school, Meg's long blonde hair and perfect breasts attracted the undivided attention of every male student. This attention was noticed by her mother, as were the looks Meg received in public from other young male admirers. Peggy became insanely jealous and over protective of her daughter and the usually happy and carefree Meg began to resent her mother's constant and overbearing, intrusive behaviour.

The second major event was the death of her mother's parents and the inheritance Peggy received, making her even more independent of the long suffering Mark.

The third event was the death of her father just before Meg's sixteenth birthday which enabled Peggy to concentrate on living the life she had once planned, convinced her dreams in society may now be achieved through her beautiful and popular daughter.

Chapter Two

Peggy enrolled Meg into one of Perth's most exclusive girls' schools and much to her mother's disgust the outgoing Meg again became an instant hit with the other girls.

Meg was at a loss as to why she was refused permission to attend parties given by the parents of other students on weekends. To her there seemed no reason for such restrictive behaviour by her mother, never had she given her any reason to distrust her. Though very popular with many boys she had neither a boyfriend nor any physical contact with men. Meg had formed a special bond with one of the girls whose parents played a pivotal role in Perth's elite, but because of Peggy's simmering jealousy was again refused permission to attend her friend's birthday party. Meg though attended without it!

This initial move into society was to be the catalyst for Meg attending parties nearly every weekend. She loved the party atmosphere and the attention of men, the romantic walks back to the boarding school facilities and the passionate good-night kisses. The awakening of her sexual desires even frightened the young Meg a little, knowing that to go too far could mean pregnancy. Just the thought of her mother's reaction to that, limited the stage she allowed her eager, would-be lovers to reach. Even so, several times when bidding one of her favourite suitors goodnight, Meg became fully aroused by the hardness of his manhood pushing against her parted legs and had

103

to fight to control herself from completely accepting her lover.

Had Meg been fully aware of the bodily functions of sexually aroused men, her mother may never have been aware of her daughter's weekend party trysts. However, on Meg's monthly weekend home, Peggy noticed semen stains on Meg's panties while sorting the washing. The resulting altercation was heated and hysterical and although Meg denied having had intercourse, she did admit to the sexual gratification she and her lovers enjoyed. Suffice to say, on returning her daughter to school on the Sunday night, Peggy gave the school hierarchy strict instructions that Meg was to never leave the confines of the school without her permission.

Meg missed the party life she really loved and which had been a great escape from her sheltered life. She missed also the attention of the men and realised that, even at such a young age, she was a very sexual person. Although disappointed, Meg settled into completing her private schooling, accepting that in order to leave the home of her mother she would have to obtain a good education and a well-paying job before she had any chance of gaining her independence.

Little did Meg realise that her mother had no such plan in mind for her daughter, having secretly booked passage on a ship to England for them both in order for Meg to attend a finishing school in the United Kingdom. Peggy had arranged to stay with family members while her daughter attended a Ladies' College and had long since decided that her daughter would not be marrying some low life in Perth, as she had done. Instead, Meg's beauty would be exploited to ensnare a gentleman of stature and importance.

When confronted with the news, Meg knew at this time in her life she had no option but to go along with her mother. Without money or job prospects, her chances on the streets of Perth were not a viable option and it had come to Meg's mind that such a trip may well have a few benefits. After years of schooling the boat voyage would be like an adventure and having heard her mother talk of England for years, at least to go and see what all the fuss was about seemed a good idea.

During the several weeks over the Christmas period while awaiting their departure date, it became quite apparent that the hostility between mother and daughter had turned into open warfare.

Peggy became obsessed with controlling her vibrant daughter and nothing Meg did or tried to do would please her. It was a great relief for Meg to walk up the gangplank at Fremantle harbour and board the ship to England. Fortunately for Meg, but an annoyance to Peggy, they had separate cabins, albeit with shared bathroom facilities between several passengers.

Meg loved the shipboard life and soon became popular with the other young passengers. On the second night, after bidding her mother goodnight, she started the nightly ritual of changing in the female restrooms and dancing the night away in the ship's ballroom, often sneaking back to her cabin just on daylight. Many a morning her mother knocked on her cabin and entered to see Meg sleeping peacefully.

It was on one of these nightly excursions that Meg met a young male passenger returning to England after an extended holiday with relatives in Australia. Having consumed too much alcohol after a night of drinking and dancing, Meg accepted her new friend's assistance back to her cabin. Once inside they began kissing passionately and fell upon the bed. Meg knew she was drunk and that this was not proper but instinctively wrapped her long legs around her partner, locking him in an alcohol-fuelled embrace.

Meg felt the hardness of his erection against her swelling womanhood, and his fingers roughly pull her panties to one side. In one thrust he entered her and immediately she broke from their deep-throated kiss, gasping in surprise and pain as he took her virginity and drove into twice again before shuddering, as he expelled his semen inside her, then rolled off. They both lay gasping for breath, Meg fully aware, from all she had learned from school friends about pregnancy, that it was possible she may have conceived. She felt ashamed of the uncontrolled urge that had overtaken her and her head began to ache.

Her lover rolled over again and holding her in another embrace kissed her gently before sitting up. As if in some kind of trance and unable to stop him, Meg allowed him to remove her panties and watched as he shed his clothes, mesmerised by the sight of his strong young body and now erect penis. He then parted her legs and pulled her dress up over her head, before unclipping her bra and gazing at her naked body. Again they became locked in an erotic union of sweaty bodies as he drove his manhood into her. Completely overcome by her pent-up passion, Meg's long-suppressed sexual frustration exploded as she wrapped her legs around her lover and rose into him with each of his deep thrusts. For the next hour or more, Meg enjoyed the fantastically uninhibited sex, completely lost in the pleasure of their union. Insatiable now and with the fire still smouldering within her, she was disappointed when her lover groaned as he climaxed and withdrew, discharging warm, sticky semen in patches over her stomach.

A strange feeling came over Meg as she watched him dress and with a wave to her, quietly slip out of her cabin. It was only then she realised the name of her lover had completely escaped her. Meg had never imagined the sexual awakening her first union would bring, but she now felt like a real woman.

Arising, she put on a dressing gown and went to the ladies' rest room. As she stood, legs apart over the toilet washing herself, she watched as a small droplet of semen dripped from her vagina. For some reason she did not feel ashamed or afraid now but relieved, even happy that she no longer thought about what her first encounter would be like. It was over and she had enjoyed the excitement of the union.

Meg returned to her cabin, picked up the crumpled clothes from the floor and slipped into some clean panties. Now that all her previous thoughts on sex had become a reality, Meg knew it would remain a large part of her womanhood and intended to enjoy her sexuality. She climbed back into bed, into the bed in which she had sexual intercourse for the first time and drifted off to sleep, to the soothing roll of the ship.

Although her partner on that night made several more approaches on the remainder of the journey, Meg chose not to have another tryst with him. He was a nice, clean-cut young man but in reality he had no attraction for her, they had simply enjoyed a night of passion and he had freed her of her virginity. Their little assignation was over now and from hereon she would choose her lovers carefully. Any man who wanted her favours would certainly have to earn the right and no-one would again delight in her sexuality on their first encounter.

Meg enjoyed the remainder of the voyage, especially the passage through the Suez Canal and a brief stop in Egypt, but was in fact relieved when they docked in London. She viewed the voyage as a big step in her life and looked forward to whatever the next may bring. Waiting on the docks for her were a distant uncle and his wife.

London was crowded and Meg missed the blue sky and clean, white sand of the beaches around Perth. In fact she became rather homesick in the first week. London was still a mess and even after two years the amount of destruction the war had created was still evident, although large amounts of reconstruction had taken place. Meg admired her British cousins who simply seemed to get on with it, trying to forget the past and rebuild new lives out of the ashes. Absorbed in her adolescent life as she was at the time, the war had seemed so far away, and now somehow Meg felt ashamed at just how lucky she had been living in Perth.

On her first day at finishing school, Meg was surprised that her fellow students seemed to view the coming year only as preparation for marriage, with no comments made of career or job prospects. Her middle-upper-class companions, as one girl jokingly put it, 'were sows being primed to meet and be served by boars'. Meg soon fathomed that any educational activity she received in the next year would be of little use to her since she had no plans to become subservient to some pompous twit. The highlight of her day soon became the regular afternoon tea the girls attended at the nearby exclusive male university, one of Britain's finest. This was of course contrived to teach the girls how to behave around upper-class young gentlemen but Meg would become bored, and instead wander out of the pavilion to watch various teams competing in several student sporting programmes.

One young man in particular caught her attention. She assumed him to be Anglo Indian. He was slightly built but very athletic as he weaved his magic on the hockey field. Meg strolled past the sports oval every Tuesday and Thursday, the two days on which her mother attended women's clubs with her new found friends to raise money for charity and to then join them in pre-planned evening functions. To Meg's relief, Peggy didn't seem to keep such a close watch on her movements now, perhaps because Meg showed no real interest in the men she met.

It was on one of these strolls that Meg caught up with the shy young man who had caught her eye and was quite surprised when he introduced himself. She found him to be friendly, articulate and a perfect gentleman. Richard King was as she thought, Anglo Indian and his parents still resided in Calcutta but he lived nearby with his grandmother while studying Industrial Engineering at the university. Meg accepted Richard's invitation to show her the sights of London the following Saturday and had the best day since arriving. This was her first real excursion around the city, taking in Piccadilly Circus, The Tower of London, Buckingham Palace and a host of other sites.

Meg was amazed at the knowledge of her guide, with whom she immediately struck a close bond, and they chatted incessantly throughout the tour. Richard treated Meg to a fine lunch in one of the many restaurants and she fast became besotted with her companion. On returning to his grandmother's house that evening Meg decided to walk the short distance to her uncle's house alone, not sure of the reception Richard might receive from her over-protective mother. As she was about to leave, an Indian woman came to the door and invited Meg in to meet Richards's grandmother, who had no doubt spied the pair talking outside on the street.

Ever the inquisitive, Meg accepted the invitation and entered the stately home. Once inside Meg gasped in amazement, beautiful drapes hung everywhere, large statues stood gracefully against some walls and beautiful Indian art covered others. Meg was so enthralled she hardly noticed the arrival of a small petite woman in a flowing gown move towards her with outstretched hand. This tiny, regal-looking woman immediately intrigued Meg.

"Hello Meg, I have heard so much about you and I must say I do agree, you are ravishing my dear. I am Sara King, Richard's grandmother" she said softly while still holding Meg's hand firmly.

"Pleased to meet you Mrs King, what a lovely home you have," responded Meg.

"Meg dearest, I still live in times past. Unfortunately the war has changed everything. The splendour of the British Raj is over I'm afraid and perhaps it's good to live in the past sometimes. My life is coming to an end, the future is with you fine young people," she replied.

"Did you find it hard to return to London Mrs King, after a life in India?" Meg asked.

"Sara please, Meg. No my dear, as I have said, times have changed and my time in the sun is over. What a great life I have led, but it is in the past. My dear servant and friend Emma looks after me here now as she has done for nearly fifty years, and you can see that my grandson gives me great pleasure," Sara told her.

Noticing her still gazing at all the beautiful objects Sara invited Meg to accompany her on a tour of the house. Meg saw immediately that it had once been a hive of activity, with old photos of past family members and memories of India everywhere. Though, when Meg was ushered into Sara's master bedroom her eyes widened and she gasped in awe at the opulent splendour. Pictures and carvings of erotic figures in various positions lined the walls and dressing tables. Beautiful mirrors hung above the bed and on the front and back walls, and there was a strong smell of incense and exotic oils wafting around the room.

111

Meg's visible change of expression indicated to Sarah her keen interest and taking her by the hand said, "One day Meg, when the time is right, I will explain all of this to you and you will understand then I'm sure."

Sara guided Meg into an adjoining bedroom, almost a replica of her room, "This is Richard's room," Sara informed her, "and speaking of Richard, he will be annoyed if we do not return for tea as we have been some time. Meg, my home is yours, please call and see me whenever possible. I find youth so lovely, it makes one feel young again and brings back a flood of wonderful memories, my dear."

Meg was unable to forget the beautiful four-poster beds with their shimmering drapes hanging to the floor. The eroticism of the place was overwhelming and it aroused her sexual fantasies.

Returning to the dining room they found Emma fussing about pouring tea into beautiful Chinese porcelain cups, which she served with small delicate sandwiches. Having immediately taken a shine to each other, Sara and Meg chatted incessantly until early evening.

When it was time to leave, Richard escorted Meg to the door. Without thinking, she bent slightly and kissed him gently, shocked and confused at the electricity between them. Meg swayed and turned, slowly walking off towards her uncle's house, her sexual arousal at a high. It was then she realised she was hopelessly in love and that Richard was the man for her.

Richard was somewhat confused when he went to say good night to his beloved grandmother. He planned to retire early and study, aware that his half-Indian ancestry meant for him to succeed he must do far better than any of his fellow students. His grandmother gestured for him to sit next to her and he knew, as in the past, this action pre-empted a quiet and confidential talk. Always the astute student, he listened intently to her advice and valued her wise counsel.

"My dear Richard," Sara quietly began, "Meg is obviously very attracted to you and I must tell you that you have here a girl whose beauty will give her the choice of any man. Her sexual vibrancy is so evident, she is like a tigress about to spring. Her unexplored passion will need your patience and all the expertise you have been taught by your mother and Emma in giving a woman pleasure. How you handle and satisfy this pent-up volcano will guide your relationship. Disappoint her and you will never hold her."

"My dear Gran," Richard began, "I think I may never have the chance to advance a relationship with Meg beyond being a good friend. I am very attracted to her but I have never actually used any of the knowledge I've gained from Mama and Emma's instruction."

"Richard answer me this, do you want Meg as a lover and perhaps your future wife?" enquired Sara.

"Why would I not fantasise about making love to her Gran? Meg is the perfect seductress with her beautiful soft skin, perfect legs and alluring breasts. Of course I desire her and would be proud to have her as my wife," he responded.

Rising from her chair Sara looked at her grandson and smiled, "Then my dear, prepare to satisfy your seductress.

113

I will have an invitation delivered to her mother inviting Meg to attend dinner and stay the night with me this coming Friday."

Richard was unable to study that evening, knowing his willpower and strength were soon to be tested. He knew too that his grandmother had given him good counsel. He would need to use all the skills his mother Aashna and Emma had taught to him in the ways of sexual gratification if he were to properly please Meg and give her the ultimate pleasure she was seeking.

Chapter Three

Meg walked home, reflecting on how even a quick kiss had caused her to want the relationship to go much further. Entering her uncle's house, she bid her mother and auntie goodnight and retired to her bedroom. She gazed at herself as she stood undressing in front of the mirror. Fully aroused, her nipples erect and almost in a trance, her hands slipped between her legs bringing forth small gasps of pleasure. It was here and now that Meg planned to seduce Richard King.

Unbeknown to Meg, the following morning a London taxi was summoned to take Sara King the short distance to Meg's uncle's home. Alighting from the cab, Sara strode to the door and knocked, happy to see it was Meg's uncle who opened it.

"I am Lady Sara King," Sara cheerfully introduced herself, "I have come in person to deliver an invitation to Meg. Such a lovely young lady I have had the pleasure to meet on a few occasions as she was walking home from college."

Sara was immediately ushered into the parlour and introduced. Peggy, upon hearing Lady Sara King had arrived with a personal invitation for her daughter, was deeply impressed.

"My dear Peggy, if I may call you that," Sara addressed Peggy, "and please call me Sara. I am most taken with your delightful daughter and wonder if I may have the

115

pleasure of her company for the weekend?"

"By all means," Peggy replied, "since you only live a short distance away and as long as Meg agrees, you have my blessing."

"Thank you Peggy," Sara beamed, "I can assure you she will have a great time."

Graciously declining an invitation to stay for morning tea, Sara explained that the taxi was waiting to take her to an important meeting. In truth Sara had no such meeting but did not want to engage in small talk with Peggy and perhaps have to lie if questioned as to exactly who lived in the house with her. On the journey home, Sara smiled, pleased with her progress. To a lady such as herself, who rose above the normal boundaries of sexuality, uniting two young people in copulation and sexual gratification, when both obviously wanted the union to occur, was simply the right thing to do.

Sara felt young again, remembering the high life her late husband and she had led in India and the sexually charged atmosphere of all the wonderful parties. Meg, in some ways, reminded her of herself in those early days, with her perfect, white, milky skin. Sensual in all aspects but innocent in many ways. Sara was sure Meg's fire had been lit and that her pent-up passion was ready to explode.

After a boring day at college, Meg, as usual, passed the university sports oval hoping to see Richard. Unfortunately though, having scanned the grounds from behind the picket fence, she was unable to locate him and her mood was sombre as she arrived home.

Her mother and auntie were both grinning as she entered

the drawing room. Beaming with pride, her mother held up the note and informed her that Lady Sara King had hand-delivered an invitation for her to spend the weekend at her stately home. Peggy went on to express her delight in her daughter making such important friends, assuring Meg that this was a step in the right direction and that in light of the invitation she and her aunt and uncle intended visiting more relatives in Scotland, leaving early Friday and returning late Monday.

Meg was elated, sure Sara had some hidden agenda, but simply smiled and wished them all a happy weekend before going straight to her bedroom. She was sure too that Sara had a very intriguing background and was determined one day to hear her life's story.

On Friday when Meg departed for college, the three travellers left for the train station on their journey to Scotland. Meg felt free and excited about the coming evening, unsure of what to expect, yet a strong sexual desire welled deep within her.

It had been a hard day at college and was a relief to pick up her small case with spare clothes and hurriedly make her way to Richard's home. Emma met Meg at the door and escorted her into the lavishly decorated drawing room where Sara sat regally in a high-backed chair, gesturing for her guest to sit on a stool to her right.

Sara greeted Meg with a bright smile and informed her that Richard would be home in an hour or so.

Holding out her hand she went on, "Firstly my dear Meg, I must apologise for arranging this weekend without your permission. I have however always considered

117

myself capable of reading and perceiving situations and am of the opinion that action is always a better option than regret."

Meg became aware of the sweet smell of incense and of the sheer garments both Sara and Emma wore, noticing their skin shone from what appeared to be sweet smelling oils. "I hope you will understand my intentions Meg," Sarah began, "you see, a woman's sexuality has to be nurtured to reach its full potential, but for many reasons some women are too afraid and hold back from reaching sexual nirvana, the ultimate experience of sexual pleasure. I can sense you are highly sexual, I can see you are beautiful in the extreme and I can tell you need to be nurtured. If for some reason you are uncomfortable please tell me so Meg but my perception is that you are not, and that a powerful force exists within you ready to be freed," Sara concluded, waiting for Meg's reaction.

Meg was enthralled, this sensuous older women completely understood her feelings. What was being said made sense to Meg and for once she felt free to express herself.

"Sara what you say is so true. I've always thought something was not right with me because of my sexuality and strong urges," Meg replied.

"My dear I felt that from the beginning," Sara explained, you see Meg, what you have between your legs can bring extreme pleasure but first you must throw away all inhibitions. What you give is what you will receive. Emma has drawn you a bath and will bathe you in essential oils and massage you, ready for you two young lovers to satisfy a lust that needs to be sated and that can only be by complete sexual exhaustion." Sara then rose from her chair and taking Meg by the hand, led her to her private bathroom where Emma waited beside a huge high-backed bath. Slowly Emma approached and sensitively removed Meg's clothes, placing them on a rack beside Sara. Meg lay back in the fragrant water while Emma sponged her gently and expertly.

Sara looked at Meg and, feeling sure she had made the right decision, continued, "Meg, I told you on your first visit that one day I would explain all this to you. The erotica and these bedrooms. Even though it is so soon, I feel now is the proper time to do so."

Meg lay back in the water, now completely relaxed and fully aware that what she had wanted was going to happen. She felt more than ready but was intrigued by Sara and knew she was to hear something so special it would have an effect on her life from here on. Over the next hour Meg was bathed, gently dried and rubbed with sensual oils, then finally shaved by the experienced Emma, becoming even more aroused as Sara began her wondrous tale.

"Meg, I will first tell you my story then that of Aashna, Richard's mother, a small and delicate 'bibi' to my son, highly trained in the art of love and pleasure, in fact her name means 'devoted to love'," Sara explained, then began.

"The East India Company advertised for wives for several hundred of their male staff in India in the hope of producing a more stable and reliant workforce. The project failed due to so few taking up the offer but those who had

119

done, found it profitable to become prostitutes and service the dozens of sex-starved men. Even though a thriving Indian service existed at the time, it was more accepted for the men to attend functions with an English lady on their arm. In time the practice changed and intermarriage was promoted again, the Company anticipating that the idea would aid integration and acceptance into Indian society. It also produced a good workforce of Anglo Indians, many of whom held high positions and helped build the empire in India, but this changed when it was considered the Anglo Indians might assist in the Independence movement in India.

Sara had been one of the first to accept the challenge. Always adventurous, she boarded a boat to India and upon arrival was offered a job in the East India Office in Calcutta. Meg was not surprised at Sara's decision. As she had explained, it was apparent to her that most of the English even when married enjoyed sexual liaisons with the highly skilled Indian women, many of whom practised on huge phalluses in order to control their pelvic muscles, giving their male clients extreme pleasure over long periods of copulation.

Unashamedly Sara admitted she had quickly become aware that unless she sexually satisfied potential partners, of whom there were many from which to choose, they would eventually be enticed to the bordellos of Calcutta and went on to explain that that's when she met Emma, her now long-time confidant, who taught her the skills of the Indian sex workers.

"Firstly my dear Meg, my apologies to you for arranging

this weekend without your permission. However I have always been capable of reading body language and sensing situations. Always too, of the opinion that action is a better option than regret."

Sara held out her hand to Meg, who was aware of the sweet smell of incense and the sheer garments both Sara and Emma wore, both also shone from what appeared to be sweet smelling oils, "I hope you will understand my intentions. You see Meg, for many reasons some women are too afraid of their sexuality and hold back from reaching the ultimate in sexual pleasure. A woman's sexuality has to be nurtured and I can see that you are highly sexual, beautiful in the extreme, a flower bud to be brought to bloom. If for some reason you are uncomfortable Meg please tell me so, but my perception is that you are not and that a powerful force exists within you ready to be freed." Sara explained and waited for Meg's reaction.

Meg was captivated, this sensuous older woman had completely understood her feelings. What was being said made sense to her and she felt free to express herself. "Sara what you say is true, I feel ready to scream, I am so frustrated. I have thought for so long now that something was not right with me because of my sexuality and strong urges," she replied.

"It was at this time I became liberated in my puritan thinking and completely enjoyed my sexuality," Sara confessed, "and from that day my sexual encounters became more than pleasure, I completely lost my inhibitions and I have never regretted having really learned the art of copulation."

121

"Emma also became my lover, skilled in the art of female erotic zones and I still have a massage and encounter with her every day. You see Meg, age is no barrier to pleasure. I chose a man and we married, living a fantastic life with servants, tea parties, wonderful trips to the mountains and a fulfilled love life. Emma and I even taught my husband, William, the art of pleasure and lovemaking and he never, as far as I know, left our bed for an outside liaison. The union produced one son."

Sara then elucidated on how Richard's father, Ian King, came to have a 'bibi', or Indian wife, at forty-five. Being overweight and awkward he would on occasion arrange with an Indian woman from a highly regarded agent, who supplied mistresses to the wealthy, to send over a woman for the evening.

On one such evening, Aashna arrived, escorted by her woman servant. As soon as Ian saw her he became infatuated and even more so after she had practised her skills on him, so expert was she in the art of pleasure. Her small delicate hands and tiny feet mesmerised him and he immediately sent the woman servant for the agent. After some haggling he purchased the tiny Aashna for his mistress and after several years she gave birth to Richard, whom both parents adored.

"I too love my daughter-in-law," Sara remarked, "so you see Meg, the family you now choose to enter regards the art of lovemaking as a skill to be embraced, enjoyed and above all to give you and your partner total sexual satisfaction. I am sure Richard, who has been taught by Emma to honour women and to never leave his lover dissatisfied, will take you to the heights of ecstasy and the complete bliss of sexual contentment that I can see you so desire."

Meg lay on a soft rug feeling the sensation of almost floating, with two courtesans in the twilight of their years preparing her for lovemaking. Emma's soft body and her small and expert hands gently massaged Meg in places one would have thought taboo, but now seemed quite normal. Meg's plan was to seduce Richard but here she was being prepared for the union. Emma straddled Meg, her soft naked buttocks rubbing gently on Meg's breasts as her tiny fingers stroked her swelling vagina, causing small waves of sensation to arch Meg's body in small spasms.

Having now become aware that the practice of preparing for copulation was accepted in many countries it seemed to Meg a far more sensible way to approach a union between lovers than to act instantly on an urge, as she had done on the ship.

Although lost as she was in pleasure and excitement, Meg was mindful that the woman gently massaging her into sexual excitement had also taught her soon-to-be lover the finer points of sexual gratification.

Meg opened her eyes to see Sara sitting cross-legged on the floor next to her. Gently picking up Meg's hand she told her, "My dear Meg, to save you any worry, Richard has been taught extreme control. He will not inseminate you, but teach you to accept finality in other places.

Sara then left the room, leaving the expert hands of Emma to seek out sexual zones Meg never knew existed.

She was so relaxed and in such a state of sexual

enlightenment, Meg fathomed that anything she had experienced thus far must just be part of total fulfilment. Emma gently rolled her over and again straddled her, massaging her buttocks. So engrossed had she become and split from actual reality, it was only when she again rolled over that she realised Richard was in the bath and smiling down at her nakedness as Emma expertly prepared him for the coming union. Meg felt so empowered by watching him gaze at her body, she opened her long legs fully displaying her womanhood, yearning for sexual gratification.

It was after Emma had gently dried Richard and massaged him sensually with tiny fingers that Meg noticed his erect penis, hard and throbbing. He took Meg by the hand and led her slowly into the bedroom. The incense, erotic decor and huge mirrors over the bed made the scene perfect. Meg felt the hard penis against her buttocks as Richard placed her gently on the bed and as they embraced on the silk sheets, Emma closed the curtains and left the room.

Chapter Four

For what seemed an eternity Richard caressed and gently stroked her, running his tongue over Meg's writhing body, bringing her to such a high state of sexual readiness she begged, no pleaded, with him to take her and only when she felt him enter her did the pleading stop. With her body arching and shaking in expectation, unable to control herself, she moaned and screamed in ecstasy as a torrent of female ejaculation gushed from her in a mind-shattering orgasm.

Richard was unable to hold back as the bucking Meg stimulated him to approach ejaculation, even though years of practice by Emma had taught him to remain in control. Gasping for breath and as his body shuddered, he withdrew before entering Meg again after he climaxed. As they lay on the bed regaining their breath and covered in sweat they were both disappointed the end had come so soon. Emma appeared silently and parting the sheer drapes, gently wiped Meg's still twitching body down with warm scented water and quickly gave Richard a sponge down before passing them both a sweet cool drink.

The floating sensation was immediate and a warm feeling enveloped Meg's soul as Richard again, to her surprise and elation, entered her. This time their union was more gentle and controlled and for what seemed like hours they both totally immersed themselves in the pleasure of each other's bodies. Twice Meg had orgasms until once again

Richard, near exhaustion and so heightened sexually by the erotic Meg, succumbed and ejaculated.

As if by magic, Emma appeared to sponge them both down, taking care when wiping Meg's still swollen vagina and massaging her with sensual oils. As Emma was about to leave, Meg heard her speak in low tones to Richard as if giving instruction.

It was now the early hours of the morning as Meg lay entwined in the arms of her lover. Although feeling tired after the long day she was still pent-up with expectation and desire and was excited to feel the hardness of Richard's erection as his penis rose again. Unlike the previous encounters, he now manoeuvred her onto her back raising her legs up under his arms so that her womanhood protruded, exposing and opening her swollen delights. He entered her gently this time, plunging to the very depths of her desire, again bringing small gasps of pleasure and as the tempo rose he rode her like a stallion, so intensely that he evoked screams of pain and pleasure.

Meg felt the sweat drip onto her breasts as her lover relentlessly plunged into her and looking at the mirror above for the first time, she was fascinated to see herself arching as he drove deep into her. She felt one last eruption coming as transfixed, she watched him ream in and out to his full extent. Bucking to meet his wild thrusts she felt the volcano about to explode. Richard withdrew, time his orgasm so intense that she felt the sticky substance hit her heaving breasts. It was the first time Meg had witnessed a male ejaculation or watched the act of copulation and she felt completely sated, her mountain top scaled, her passion waning.

Meg's desires were satisfied and now instead of sensual responses to touching, she was tender, her fire extinguished. She knew though she'd reached such heights with their union that she would be unable to settle for anything less in future encounters.

Although exhausted, Meg felt the blanket being softly pulled up over her as she drifted into a deep sleep, wrapped in the arms of her lover. As both slept soundly Sara closed the door, the spectacle she observed had justified her decision. She intended, with the expert help of Emma, to now train Meg in the art of satisfying Richard. The tigress had been satisfied, although during the night Sara did have reservations, fully aware the fire she had started in Meg was perhaps greater than even she anticipated.

As morning came the patter of rain and wind beat against the roof. Warm and still entwined in each other's arms, it was only when the ever silent Emma gently woke them that Meg fully comprehended what had taken place during the long night. She was astounded that they had entered the bed between 6 and 7pm and didn't get to sleep until after 4am. It had taken nearly ten hours to satisfy their lust. Gazing at the beautiful body of her lover, she could see no future without him, no other man would ever satisfy her desires.

Meg was starving. They had skipped the evening meal, so engrossed was the household in the coming union that no-one mentioned food. Meg wondered if this had been planned but, covering themselves in the exotic dressing gowns of pure silk, they entered the dining room. She was immediately intrigued by both Emma and Sara laying on huge pillows on a soft rug next to the coal fire, the glow and warmth from the heater making the scene surreal. In the centre was a low table covered in sweet meats and other delights along with a huge tea-pot and four beautifully decorated cups. Smiling at her guest Sara indicated for Meg to lie next to her and as she did so was surprised that Sara gave her a warm hug. "You look ravishing my dear, did the stallion satisfy the tigress in you?" she asked.

"Most assuredly," Meg replied, "but I fear from now on she will expect the same in the future."

"Ah, then Meg perhaps you must also learn skills that will keep your stallion in the home stable," Sara suggested.

"Absolutely," Meg agreed, as she ate heartily of the exotic foods set before her while Emma served the sweet tea. Meg found the whole situation unreal although it all seemed natural to the others as they lay on the soft rugs, eating and recalling intriguing stories of India and great times past.

While in London Richard still helped his father by meeting with trading partners and conducting business on his behalf. His father now felt more at home in Calcutta and hated the trips back home to England. Sara reminded Richard of a lunchtime appointment they'd been unable to cancel at such late notice and suggested, as the weather was so foul, that Meg stay at home with her two older confidants in his absence. All thought this a good idea, especially the still exhausted Meg.

Laying against the soft pillows in such opulence and now

comfortable with her older courtesans, Meg somehow felt more at peace than at any other time in her life. Richard excused himself to dress and when he bent over to kiss Meg as he bade them all farewell, she still felt a tingle at his contact. After he left Meg drifted off in the arms of Sara, who was also besotted with her son's find and unable to quite comprehend how of all suitors, Meg had chosen Richard.

Waking refreshed, Meg found lunch on the table and the still slumbering Sara close beside her. She realised of course that both Sara and Emma must have been awake most of the night too and that it was more than possible they had watched the proceedings. The actual thought of that pleased her somehow, as it was their planning that produced the evening she had so much enjoyed.

Gently Emma woke Sara and both she and Meg washed their hands in the bowl offered by her, before drying their hands. Again Meg enjoyed a wonderful meal while reclining in the luxuriant setting. Sara and Meg chatted incessantly, the older woman regarding her as a protégé and Richard's future wife. After the meal Sara became somewhat serious and looking at Meg remarked, "Meg last night was just the start. I knew a fire raged inside you, but be assured it is not out, it is dormant. Richard may have sated your passion but it is only temporary and you will undoubtedly want more. However, in saying that, you must also learn to satisfy your man, for if you do not, others will. It is only by mutual gratification that true enlightenment can be reached. Emma and I want to show you the tricks of the great courtesans and train you to become a complete lover."

Emma walked over to a huge elephant tusk covered by a brightly coloured velvet cloth. Removing the cover, Emma pushed the tusk carefully towards the two women. Intrigued now, Meg noticed three round holes in the tusk beneath which on the stand was an ornamental wooden box with intricate carving. Opening the box Emma removed three phalluses, placing one in each hole, all a perfect fit and ranging in size. The first about six inches, the second eight and the last quite thick and ten inches. Meg was awestruck, unsure of what was to come next.

"Now Meg, Emma will demonstrate how with practice a woman can control her pelvic muscles and we will teach you this once the soreness of your vigorous love making has passed," Sara told the wide-eyed Meg.

Standing up and dropping her negligee to the ground, Emma rubbed oil between her legs and in a trance like state, legs apart, lowered herself onto the first of the glistening, ivory carved phalluses. Meg watched amazed as the head slowly disappeared into her vagina. Then, when only an inch in, Emma tightened her muscles and slowly lifted the object from the tusk until it completely disappeared within her. She then walked up to Sara and as she held the carved box open, Emma gently squeezed the object out, placing it carefully back into its position. She repeated the same on the second larger phallus, only this time pleasuring herself first into a trance, lowering herself up and down while gyrating her hips ever so slowly and sensually. Meg's eyes were riveted to the scene.

Aroused by what she saw, Meg's mouth felt dry and

she drank more sweet tea before asking Sara, "Why are Indian women so sexual?" adding, I would love to do such things. I can imagine the pleasure I could then give Richard."

Sara replied as she arose, dropping her dressing gown to stand naked, arousing Meg even more. "I will show you Meg, all women are capable of learning total pleasure both for themselves and their lovers."

Meg was now focused on the larger phallus as the tiny Sara, still with firm breasts and buttocks, mounted the huge phallus and in one flowing motion with hips gyrating, slid completely down to the base, displaying great pleasure as she consumed the monster. Rising again slowly, Sara had full control over the ivory object on which she had impaled herself.

Meg watched mesmerised as Sara too placed the phallus back into its position in the carved box, her vagina closing as its gigantic bulbous head slipped easily from her total control. Now aware that both women enjoyed total sexual liberation in their lives, Meg made up her mind to learn from them how to not just enjoy her sexuality, but to give her lover consummate pleasure.

So taken with the moment, Meg slowly rose and dropping her cover to the floor, walked as if she too were in a trance, to the huge glistening monster. Spreading her legs she impaled herself on it, just as Sara had done. The act took her breath away but the sensation was electric and with eyes glazed she finally accepted the entire length, stretching her muscles and sending waves of sensation throughout her entire body. Although she tried to hold and lift the huge cock, it slipped from her each time. The scene though was so erotic and sensual that Meg stood shaking, feeling almost empty after a mind-blowing orgasm, before collapsing back onto the floor.

All three lay naked, the fire dancing in patterns over their nakedness. Meg was determined to keep practising and, under the tutelage of her older confidants, to learn the art of true sexual liberation and of giving and receiving ultimate pleasure.

Emma heated water and the three enjoyed a hot bath. The two older women massaged and rubbed exotic oils on the nymph who had entered their lives, both aware that they had started the sexually charged Meg on her journey to total sexual gratification.

Again Emma prepared a hot bath when Richard returned cold and hungry, but this time invited Meg to dry and massage her lover. Seated backwards over him, Meg enjoyed the pleasure of slowly rubbing Richard with the sweet smelling oils and tenderly stroked his scrotum and rising penis. Unable to control herself Meg rose up and slammed down on him while both older women watched on. Now it was Meg's turn and, riding her stallion with such passion, she brought Richard quickly to climax and he withdrew tipping her gently forward, their encounter culminating in an explosion of semen over her buttocks. Meg sat, chest rising and falling gasping for air, frightening even herself by the untamed and raw sexual urges that flowed through her very being. In this home her inhibitions had been cast away and her true feelings had finally been allowed to manifest themselves.

This was to be the scenario for the weekend. Eating, sleeping and engaging totally in sex. Both she and Richard fine-tuned each other's wants and needs and Meg's years of sexual frustration were finally liberated.

Dressing for college on the Monday morning Meg reflected on it being the first time in three days she had actually worn clothes. All day on the Sunday, with rain lashing the house, all four had remained naked as they laughed, ate and slept in the sexual ambience created by both older women. The scent of sexually charged females permeated the air and despite being watched by the other two, Meg several times entwined with Richard in long, controlled copulation. Total inhibition now seemed natural. Meg had accepted one last lingering kiss from Richard and warm hugs from Sara and Emma, her soul mates. She loved them both dearly and they in turn worshipped her, a young goddess who had entered their lives.

Chapter Five

All that day at college, listening to the teachers instilling in their charges a perfect world that no longer existed, Meg day-dreamed about her time with Richard, Emma and Sara. Especially the two liberated older women. She really did love them both and was excited about the coming weeks, fully intent on learning everything they shared with her in their lessons of a very different kind. She was fully aware that very few women would ever experience the sexual gratification she had enjoyed on the weekend.

Aware that Richard had two more years of study before graduating, the thought of leaving England to return home troubled her now that she had experienced his expert lovemaking. Not to be near him was unthinkable, and since there were a further eight months of her college course to run she determined somehow to find a way to stay until he completed his studies.

Returning home that evening she was confronted by her mother about her weekend. Meg not wanting to seem too enthused just said she had enjoyed Sara's company and that she was a lovely lady. Peggy whinged about the weather in Scotland and everything else, just as Meg had expected. Actually Meg felt sorry for her mother for the first time, aware that if given the chance, Peggy too would have excelled in the sexual stakes. Meg knew though that beneath her exterior there beat a bitter and frustrated woman and that her frustrations had lost her the chance of true love and passion. The only difference between Sara and Peggy was that one liberated herself and the other denied herself her true feelings.

Meg knew her dear father was sexually naive and that due to Peggy's disinterest, simply relieved himself into her, their union lasting a few brief seconds. Meg smiled thinking of her marathon sessions and her lover's determination to satisfy her desires. She couldn't understand why her mother, still rather attractive even now, never sought the company of other men. Surely, Meg thought, any healthy woman must have some urges, musing that Sara was proof age was no barrier to sexual feelings.

Several times that week, Meg dropped into Sara's home and spent at least two hours eagerly learning both how to enjoy coitus and also to satisfy and make her lover's experience more enjoyable.

In one conversation Sara, who was a little troubled by her treatment of Meg, explained her reasons to the young woman she now adored. "Meg my dear, many would consider what I have done is really training and procuring a sexual toy for my grandson and yes, perhaps for my own fetish reasons. In fact, and I again have to confess, that watching your first kiss, I knew you would eventually seduce him. I also knew my grandson would never be able to resist such an erotic nymph and I thought it preferable that the inevitable union be in a controlled and safe environment. I envisaged your pent-up passion creating a liaison in an unsafe environment and that should any Englishman from the University have come across you together, the result may have been horrific.

You see Meg, my dear, we live in a false world of stupid expectations. At the very finishing school you attend, eventually you will have a lesson in sexual practices for young ladies. A spinster who has never seen a man's penis will tell you to never allow a gentleman to go too far in the relationship before marriage. That when married you must always be in bed waiting for your hard-working husband, no matter what time of night he returns home, and after the sexual act you must quietly leave the matrimonial bed and clean yourself up. To show any passion or enjoyment would qualify you as a woman of poor morals. That is why Meg, two at least, of the girls at your college have left because of pregnancy. The stupid teachers live in a world of unreality. Far better to teach the girls sexual liberation and how to avoid pregnancy. More desirable marriages would eventuate and those poor girls would learn to enjoy their sexuality. In all societies, many strange sexual activities are regarded as normal. Many men enjoy young boys, others go with animals and others use even more deviant practices, while many enslave women through religion. That is why, when I first saw your sparkling eyes and was aware of your pent-up passion, I made it my mission to teach you all I have experienced. To nurture and shape you so that in your life you may float in a world of sexual liberation and enjoy your body unashamedly. Coitus is the greatest gift of life, if it is given freely and unconditionally."

Meg agreed and only then remembered that two girls had in fact travelled overseas on short notice, one in particular was a friend. She was a pretty, outgoing girl and Meg suddenly felt sad for her. What a pity she had never met someone like Sara to guide her through her sexual urges. Instead, now she was an outcast, whispered about by so-called high society, while the man responsible would have no doubt been slapped on the back by his colleagues and regarded as some kind of a stud, when in fact the oaf possibly had only a short interlude with the girl.

Four months passed and true to Sara's prediction, Miss Pringle-Jones-Smith gave her talk on the sexual conduct expected of high-class young women. It was also by this time that Sara and Emma had imparted all their knowledge and skills to her and it was now up to her through practice to hone those skills. At least twice a week Meg stayed overnight at Sara's, during which time she and Richard reached new and exciting levels of sexual pleasure. One morning while Meg was dressing for college, Sara entered the bedroom after Richard had left for university. She placed a beautiful ivory carved depiction of two lovers around Meg's neck. Encased in solid gold and on an exquisite gold chain, it hung between her breasts, and she loved it.

"A present for my pupil, who has, I know, reached the heights of sexual enlightenment. I can show you no more, you have made an old woman happy, and through you I have again lived my years of pleasure," Sara told her with tears in her eyes. Both women embraced, a special bond now existing between them, then to Meg's surprise, Sara added, "Enjoy many lovers."

"But Sara, I would never think of making love to anyone

137

but Richard," Meg replied.

"My dearest, please remembers this. Only in a perfect world do we always achieve our dreams. Sometimes fate intervenes. I hope so with all my being your wish comes true, but if not, you will have a special place in my heart forever. I love you dearly and see myself in you. Sadly, unlike us, very few women have such strong feelings and the strength of will to achieve the satisfaction they desire."

Meg and Richard spent many a happy Sunday walking, picnicking and making love. Both like finely tuned instruments, their unions created perfect notes as they pleasured each other for hours during many long nights.

The end of the year was approaching and Meg was aware from the many discussions she'd had with Richard that he would go with Emma and Sara to Calcutta for the holiday season, and knew too that Peggy had booked fares home via Egypt for the two of them. Following long conversations, the lovers, in consultation with Sara, decided Richard would finish his studies, then join Meg in Australia to see if the relationship was still strong enough for them to marry. Both Richard and Meg made a solemn pledge to write at least once a week. Meg secretly planned though to save up and return to England the following year, if at all possible.

The presentation evening and coming-out ball for Meg's college approached. It was considered a big event with the University Head Professor presenting each graduate into society. Meg was a little unimpressed, thinking her life was perfect having found her soul mate and considered the whole affair rather stupid. However, at her mother's cajoling, Meg chose a beautiful full-length gown and was even herself a little astounded with her appearance. Her long blonde hair was beautifully styled and her gorgeous gown absolutely moulded her body to perfection. Meg smiled when everyone commented on her figure. Little did they know that months of stomach-muscle training and athletic sexual activity, coupled with long walks with Richard, had made her trim and taut.

When Peggy questioned her as to her intended escort, much to Peggy's annoyance, Meg simply explained that one of the university students had agreed to be her companion for the evening and refused to elaborate further.

Richard had in fact put his departure for India off for a week so he could spend it with Meg and to be her escort at the ball. The evening arrived with much fanfare and Meg caused a sensation among every hot-blooded young man when she swept into the great hall. Seated in a balcony above the dance floor, Peggy noticed Sara King in an alcove opposite with an Indian woman seated directly behind her.

All the girls were lined up and with formalities over, Peggy was horrified when Meg held out her hand to a young Anglo Indian student, even though he looked stunning in his tuxedo. The band struck up and while most couples awkwardly waddled to the floor and tried to look as if they could dance, everyone was enthralled as Meg and her partner glided like two graceful swans around the dance floor. Many of the crowd, including Sara King and her Indian companion, clapped loudly and cheered the glamorous young couple.

Even Peggy's relatives stood and applauded, while she just silently fumed. So embarrassed was she that at the interval she made the excuse of a violent headache and left. Peggy was now fully aware that both Meg and her partner had met before and knew too, by their body language and closeness as they danced, that they were certainly more than acquaintances.

Although many other young men vied for a dance with Meg she gracefully declined their requests. This evening was for her and Richard, all else was inconsequential. Even though initially Meg considered the whole thing a bit stupid, now caught up in the atmosphere, gliding around the dance floor in the arms of her lover, the evening became enchanted and was something she would never forget.

Meg had arranged with her mother to stay at Sara's and it was well after midnight when they both fell onto the huge bed, clothes strewn on the floor. The evening had been sensuous, the atmosphere electric and they knew this was to be their last night together for some time.

Time and time again during the night their passion boiled over, as expending all their sexual skills, they enjoyed the pleasure of multiple orgasms and it was only total exhaustion that broke their coupling. Perhaps it was the thought of potentially not seeing each other for months that they were reluctant to release each other from their union but as daylight began to creep across the giant bed, both totally spent, drifted off to sleep.

Meg heard Emma's quiet voice as she gently shook Richard awake, "Please, the taxi will be here in one hour to take us to the boat, we must hurry." Turning, tears in her eyes, Meg faced Richard and they embraced, not knowing when they would be together again.

Emma, with a tear running down her cheek, stood silently holding a dressing gown in front of her. As Meg stepped out of bed, Emma placed the gown around her naked body as always, but this time placed her arms around her as well and whispered, "Such beauty is like that of the lotus flower, never let a man drink the nectar unless he deserves it. Please remember, I will always be your friend."

With that, Emma turned and left the room, both knew to delay was to miss Richards's departure on the steamer for India. Meg, her heart beating so hard she thought she would die, struggled to dress, her mind in turmoil. For the past ten months she and Richard had been constant friends and lovers, to be parted was unthinkable.

Sara approached Meg, she too with tears streaming down her proud face, "Meg you are the daughter I never had, I love you unconditionally. Until we meet again, soon I hope, please take care of yourself. Your beauty and passion is a great gift, always use your skills wisely."

Sitting at a table trying to drink the tea Emma had served, Meg in a daze stared at the cases of luggage piled at the door ready for the taxi that would take her beloved away to a foreign land. Sara was unusually quiet, a close bond had been forged, Meg was now family. Emma cleared and covered the table, just as the other furniture had been covered days before.

It began to rain as the taxi pulled up outside, adding to the sadness of the occasion. Sara and Emma embraced

Meg one last time. Sara for once was stuck for words, so emotional that she seemed to have been robbed of her vibrancy.

Richard and Meg squeezed each other tightly, both with tears streaming down their faces. "Meg, I will always love you and one day soon we will be reunited. I promise I will write to you every day, you are the essence of my life," Richard said, choking back emotion so strong it broke Meg's heart.

With that the taxi drove off, unable to delay any longer. Meg stood in the cold drizzle of London, a forlorn figure. Her last memory was of Richard waving goodbye from the front seat and of Sara and Emma still crying, looking out the rear window, as they disappeared into the heavy mist.

It was then Meg noticed a second taxi that apparently Sara had called and paid for to take her home, although it was only a short walk. Even the taxi driver was affected by the scene and helped the distraught Meg into the back. Arriving at her Uncle's home, Meg was absolutely beside herself but thanked the kind driver as she waved him away. Opening the front door, she walked in to find her mother waiting with arms folded. Peggy was alone in the home, which was some solace to Meg, as she yelled, "Really Margaret did you have to cause such a scene at the ball last night, it was such a spectacle!"

Meg, no longer caring, replied, "Mum, if you are talking about my escort for the evening, he is my lover and has been for nearly the entire year I have been here. As a matter of fact I bet I had more orgasms last night than you have had in your life! One day, when he finishes university, I will be his wife. I love him more than life itself." With that Meg stormed off into her bedroom, slamming the door behind her and falling onto the bed, sobbing uncontrollably, completely devastated.

Peggy stood stock-still, mouth open in complete bewilderment. She knew her worst nightmare had happened at four o'clock that afternoon when the newspapers were delivered. The same story in all the papers along with a photo of the young couple on the front pages, simply read,

'At last night's Debutante Ball some of London's finest young women graduated from Ladies' College and were presented to the Lord Mayor and distinguished guests. Among those were Lady Sara King whose grandson Richard King was lucky enough to be escort to Margaret Jackson, a striking beauty from Perth in Western Australia.'

Peggy was livid. Now that she knew why they had been so obviously at ease with each other, she fumed as she recalled giving Meg permission to stay at the home of Sara King, recognising that in a way she herself had created and unknowingly nurtured the whole affair. Although no further words were spoken on the matter Peggy was determined to somehow end the relationship. Crushed that her glamorous daughter was in love with an Anglo Indian, it seemed to her bigoted mind that the year of finishing school was an absolute waste of time and money.

Meg never left her room that day but simply lay in a foetal position, her heart aching at the thought of Richard sailing so far away. Even the idea of a holiday in Egypt

143

on the trip back to Australia meant nothing.

On boarding the ship the following evening, Meg immediately headed for her cabin, and clutching the ivory carving around her neck, exhausted and traumatised, fell into a troubled sleep.

Chapter Six

Sara sat quietly, as did all those in the taxi. For days she had agonised over the parting that had just taken place. This was to be the first time in her life that careful planning had not been able to produce a satisfactory outcome. Her choices were to have taken Meg with her and create a scandal of majestic proportions, or take the path she realistically knew she had to. Sara felt old, as if a light had been extinguished from her life and looking at her loyal companion Emma she saw great sadness in her also. As for Richard, she was aware he was hopelessly in love with Meg but, not one to ever show great emotion, he sat in silence and she knew it would take some time for him to return to his normal self, if in fact, he ever did.

On reflection, Sara couldn't deny that the youthful sexuality and beauty of Meg had reinvigorated her and rekindled times of great passion in her past. She now however felt the fire going out and a feeling of emptiness enveloped her like a dark cloud. Never before had aging crossed her mind, but watching Meg's young and athletic body during lovemaking made Sara realise her own youth had long since passed.

Even though her little group had always enjoyed the boat crossings to India, this trip seemed different. All three felt as though a large part of their lives had disappeared and on the third night Sara finally broached the subject. As Richard sat on the bed talking to Emma, Sara said,

145

"Richard I feel I have let you down but I saw no other way. For us to take someone's daughter without permission would have been a terrible thing and perhaps one day, even Meg would have regretted it. I doubt you will ever again have the chance to meet and marry such a delectable child. Meg is a beauty in the extreme who loves you unconditionally, a nymph who in the act of copulation knows no boundaries. However, having said all that, common sense must prevail. Write to her regularly, it will be a good test of her loyalty. Use the separation to prove her bond with you then, when you finish studying go to Australia and marry her. My wish too is, like you, to see her again. I also miss her greatly."

Richard didn't respond but simply nodded in agreement, aware his grandmother was right as always. Emma opened the sheet drawing him into the bed next to her and feeling her warmth, as in the past, he drifted off into sleep. He determined to work hard and finish his studies. Aware their fortune was diminishing, as were those of many of the older families in England, how could he keep Meg unless he graduated?

Two weeks later, after a family reunion one evening upon their arrival in Calcutta, Aashna approached Sara, with whom she always had an open and honest relationship. Conscious of how people's reactions to conversation can indicate feelings, Aashna had become worried about her son. Although always quiet and reserved, he seemed more serious and she had a feeling something had taken place in the last year that had affected him greatly. She mentioned her concerns to Sara and then listening to her and Emma as they told her the full story, not hiding anything, the reserved Aashna, herself a devotee of sexual satisfaction, felt deeply saddened. She knew the passage to true love with another person was a hard road, even impossible for many. Aashna herself had never experienced it, having simply been trained as a tool for men's sexual fantasies. Although her husband had been kind to her and she had led a good life, she knew she had been traded for money, like any commodity. Aashna when shown the newspaper photo of the couple on their last night, gasped at the radiance of the happy pair and wept silently for her son. It was at this time they all three decided to assist him in any way humanly possible to marry the girl he desired.

In a moment of mother and son togetherness in the garden one evening, Aashna, the tiny woman who gave him life, spoke to her son about Meg. "My son, Sara and Emma have told me everything and I have lived your heartache. I have seen the photo of you at the ball with your sweetheart and I tell you now, such beauty and poise are rare. I see why you desire her so. I pray that I may give you a big wedding when you finish your studies and that you will have many fine children. My life would then be fulfilled and I will continue to pray every day that our dreams come true."

Richard replied, "Thank you Mother. What you and Grandmother counsel is good advice. I will finish my studies and then travel to Australia to bring Meg home as my wife. I can never take another woman. All would disappoint. Once one has experienced perfection, nothing else compares."

147

The two months in India soon passed as Richard continued to help in the family business, worried though as to his father's deteriorating health. He was morbidly obese from eating and drinking too much, short of breath and so unfit that a small walk to the car and warehouse each day exhausted him. Aashna had informed Sara and Emma he no longer came to her room and even though she massaged him, he was unable to seek sexual gratification, his desires had gone. Thinking her husband's lack of desire was her fault, Aashna felt inadequate until Sara explained that age and ill-health could destroy some men's libidos. Sara too knew that 'all good things come to an end' but was pleased at least that Meg had given her some extended sexual feelings. Her presence in the home had aroused her senses.

The trip back to England and return to the English home was an uneventful affair but Richard soon perked up when he found that several letters from Meg awaited him. He was confused however when she indicated her disappointment at not receiving his promised letters. In the two months he had posted over thirty letters and Sara had also sent some small gifts and cards.

Again, he checked the address, as did Sara, more than a little confused as even Meg's letters had the return address exactly as the one they had used. Shortly after, another incident occurred, that for the time being, changed many things. A message arrived informing them that Sara's son Ian, Richard's father, had died of a massive heart attack.

Sara was beside herself with grief. On top of losing Meg, now her son had died. It took several weeks and a deferral of Richards's studies for one year, in order for him to return to India to finalise the Estate and on Sara's insistence, to bring Aashna to England. Sara was proud of Richard as he immersed himself in the sad task of selling the last of the family property in India and packing many cartons of family treasures for the return voyage to England. Richard wrote long letters to Meg telling her of his family's misfortune and the deferral of his studies. He suggested in many that she come to England at the end of the year because of the changed circumstances, and get married.

He would have gone to Australia to collect her himself, but circumstances and family responsibility at this time stopped him from doing so. It was even more apparent he had to finish his studies to support the last of his family. After settlement of all debts, very little funds still existed and it was only Sara's money now that kept the family going. This caused Richard to work even harder in order to graduate. Not one day went past without him thinking of Meg returning to England. In his dreams he still felt her near and he could smell her sensuality, the longing for her nearly drove him insane.

Even though the address was checked on every letter he sent, Meg's correspondence, now further apart, still conveyed desperation that she had not heard from him. Richard started sending telegrams, but still her letters indicated no contact.

Richard was torn between loyalty to his family and finishing his studies, or to travelling to Australia to see Meg. However their diminishing financial position now made that an impossibility. There was no way he could abandon his family and leave university. He simply had no choice, having already lost one full year of study. Sara even suggested selling the family home and all its treasures in order for him to go and find Meg, but he flatly refused. It was his responsibility, his mission in life, to above all else see the three women he loved so much, stay in the family home.

Chapter Seven

On the voyage to Egypt, even Meg, in such a state of heartbreak, soon realised that to keep up such self-punishment would not help the situation. Instead, she decided to return home and find a job, and saving as quickly as possible to return to England. Meg was fully aware her mother would offer no financial assistance having closed all doors to any relationship with her. Although, upon reflection she accepted that there never had really been one anyway. Sara and Emma had been closer as a family with her than anyone else in her entire life.

Nothing she had done, or achieved in her life to this stage, had pleased her mother. She was always critical of anything she said or did. Meg decided upon her return home, not only would she find a job but she would move out on her own, or perhaps share a flat with someone. The idea pleased her and she looked forward to seeing the sunshine of Perth and catching up with girlfriends once again.

Under different circumstances, Meg would have perhaps enjoyed the holiday in Egypt, exploring the pyramids, sailing in a felucca on the Nile and shopping in the souks of Luxor. On several occasions Meg became sick of the attention showed her by the local men, who if given the chance, tried to fondle her breasts or buttocks. Even Peggy, who had dressed in light fitting dresses because of the hot climate, attracted heavy attention. Possibly in

151

different times, both may have taken the attention a little less seriously but due to the circumstances of the past, neither viewed the constant fondling as appropriate. The only high point of the excursion was the interest in travel it inspired in Meg and in later years she would reminisce about the experience of travelling in interesting and different cultures.

Both however, seemed in high spirits as they boarded the next ship back to Fremantle. Meg had to share with Peggy on this leg of the trip but she still enjoyed the entertainment and a few dances with admirers before retiring to their cabin each evening. On several occasions she dreamt of dancing the night away with Richard in London and a few tears trickled down her face onto her pillow. Even though that was only a few short weeks ago, it seemed like an eternity.

Tired of their constant altercations Meg made some sort of truce with Peggy and carried on as normally as possible, convinced there was no future in making both their lives a misery. With the resilience of youth, Meg intended to make the most of her situation. Madly in love and indeed lust, with Richard, who had taken her to the heights of eroticism, she even now she dreamed of their next meeting, whenever that may be, firmly believing she had found her soul mate and life partner.

Meg had conjured up an image of home after a long absence, in this case fourteen months, but was to find on arrival in Fremantle that it was blowing a gale and rain was bucketing down. By the time they had passed Customs and collected their luggage, both she and Peggy felt tired in the extreme. It was not until midnight that the taxi arrived outside their home and so leaving the cases in the dining room they decided to retire for the night. Meg was happy to again be in her own bed and immediately drifted off to sleep.

Their next-door neighbours, an elderly couple from Italy and not very fluent in English, had offered to take care of the house and upon Peggy and Meg's imminent arrival had freshly made up the beds and left the key under the doormat. When Meg finally awoke at ten o'clock in the morning the rain had stopped and looking out her bedroom window she was happy to see her late father's garden perfectly manicured, the neighbours had obviously taken great pride in their responsibilities. Meg ran to the kitchen eager to see if her mother had collected the mail from next door. Peggy had in fact been over early for the mail and to deliver some gifts she had bought for the neighbours by way of thanks and in appreciation of their kindness. She was seated at the table reading anything she considered of importance. Enthusiastically Meg requested her mail but Peggy, shaking her head, informed her that no letters had come for her.

Meg was devastated. Surely by now Richard would have written. She had posted several letters to him, he was always in her thoughts. With tears welling in her eyes Meg turned and made her way back to her bedroom. She was confused, heartbroken and even a little annoyed that he had not kept his promise. Inconsolable, Meg sobbed for some time, even her appetite had gone and curled up on the bed, she felt all alone, completely abandoned, her world at an end.

Peggy knew Meg had only left her room once that day, for a toilet stop and to have a glass of milk. Despite seeing her distressed state she offered no condolences and just ignored her.

In a long letter to Richard she pleaded that, if indeed he had changed his mind and did not really love her, to please end her nightmare now. To Sara, having shared secrets of subjects taboo and above all else a relationship treasured by both, or so Meg thought, she wrote imploring her to 'please talk to Richard'.

Early the following morning Meg caught a ferry into the Perth business district and posted the two letters, kissing both as she placed them into the letterbox. Meg would have preferred to speak to them than write, but her mother did not have a phone. For some reason she refused to connect to the service that had arrived in her suburb after her father's death. In absolute desperation she sent a telegram to Richard too, also imploring him to contact her.

Having planned to find accommodation Meg was astute enough to realise at this stage financially that was impossible, so on the spur of the moment decided to see if there was any work available. Luckily one of the larger fashion houses had two vacancies for front line staff and as Meg entered the store manager's office he was immediately taken with her presentation. Then when she mentioned she had just finished Ladies' College in London, she was hired on the spot. Meg started work the following day and commuted home to her mother nightly. Starting at eight o'clock in the morning, her duties were to display new products, to clean and to prepare to open. Closing time was five o'clock. It would take an hour each way by bus and ferry to and from her workplace. Meg fitted into her new position like a 'duck to water' and with her outgoing, bubbly personality and good looks she became quite a hit with all the customers. In later life she was to reason that the work had come at just the right time. Until then she had been all alone but now several of the established clients specifically requested her to serve them.

Every night Meg looked for any letters in the day's mail without success but still, for six months, she wrote weekly. In the end she accepted that for whatever reason she had been shunned and every night wondered why. Had she been so inadequate? Had Richard met someone else? Had his father, like her own mother, insisted on putting a stop to the relationship? It was at this point, to ease her shattered ego, and perhaps for her sanity that she chose the latter. Yes, to Meg, that was the answer, somehow it gave her some closure. She immersed herself in her work, spending longer hours than any other staff member and after closing time arranging new displays in a bid to simply forget. Meg had no desire to meet men or pursue a relationship. Her great fire and passion had ebbed. In her troubled mind she felt she had been inadequate and even with the experience of heightened sexual pleasure that Sara and Emma had imparted to her, she felt a failure as a woman.

The store was opening a new branch in the expanding Fremantle district and invited Meg to be the manager of

Women's Fashion. She was thrilled and it gave her ego a much-needed boost. In partnership with a fellow worker who was also relocating, Meg found a nice three-bedroom house for rent nearby.

Peggy did not seem to be too upset at Meg's departure and simply wished her well. To Meg it was a relief to at last have freedom. Her chains to the dominant mother had been severed and she felt as if a new era, no, a new start, had begun. The move and added responsibility so soon for such a young person may have been tough for some, but not for Meg. In a very short time her store was leading all others in the fashion department. New suburbs had crept south from Perth bringing new and younger clients and they just flocked to it. Perhaps in the reaches of her mind that some mail may still arrive, Meg visited her mother monthly. Every visit seemed hard work and exhausting and in time became shorter and further apart, even Meg's great successes did not seem to please the bitter Peggy.

Weekends now became enjoyable for Meg, sailing with friends to Rottnest Island and lunching in the many restaurants that began to appear in the wharf precinct. Meg had many admirers, although none were able to break through the shield she had enveloped around herself, so badly had she been hurt. No thoughts of a relationship even entered her mind. Time moved on, as did life. Meg became settled and then promoted to buyer for all of the West Australian stores. This meant trips interstate and soon all thoughts of a future with Richard disappeared into the mists of time.

It was on a trip home by aircraft from Adelaide that Meg found herself seated next to a young man from Perth who worked for Western Power and had been to a course in Adelaide. During the trip they found they had a lot in common and after years of no male company, Meg's interest was renewed. Paul Young was a nice, quiet sort of fellow and before the flight ended they had exchanged telephone numbers.

Arriving home, Meg was disgusted with herself for finding it hard to erase thoughts of Paul from her mind. He had certainly rekindled her interest in men and having phoned and arranged to pick her up on the Saturday of the following weekend, they enjoyed a drive to Rockingham and a picnic on the beach. Paul intrigued Meg and with his beautiful blue eyes, blonde hair and easy nature he enthralled her, yet still she was cautious. He was also four years younger than Meg but seemed older because of his steady, caring behaviour. Four months of dating ensued, Meg was taking it slowly this time. Paul never forced the issue, even though Meg realised he wanted to take their relationship much further. It was on a wet Saturday night as they sat in a restaurant in Mandurah after driving back from the Margaret River that a tired Meg suggested they stay the night at the motel opposite. Feigning surprise, Paul instantly agreed. Meg had made her decision and that night they became lovers. Over the next few months Meg guided Paul in the art of pleasing her as a woman and, being a keen student, they became inseparable. Meg realised Richard would always have a place in her heart but also that life goes on and her new relationship filled a large void in her life. She had come full circle. Although Paul had used condoms they had several times come off during extended lovemaking and on a few occasions their passion overcame good judgement. Within four months Meg found she was pregnant. Paul was elated and Meg, although surprised, was not unhappy at the prospect of having a child. They decided that as Meg had to go to Adelaide, Paul would accompany her, since this was how they had first met. Arrangements were made and in a quiet registry office they were married and returned home as husband and wife. Meg resigned from work when seven months pregnant and as both she and Paul were astute savers they were able to purchase a new home at Rockingham in which to start their married life. Meg loved children and when a bouncing baby boy arrived, for the first time in her life, she had a stable family. Paul was a loving husband and good provider, spending all his spare time with the family and working around the house. Meg never reached the heights of sexual bliss with Paul as she had with Richard, but the intimacy made her feel wanted and she knew he adored her. To her, this was more than sufficient. Time passed and three more fine sons arrived making the household a bustling hive of activity, with Meg attending school functions and watching with pride as the boys excelled in sporting events. Meg settled into a happy family life and all past events faded with time. She had visited her mother after the birth of each infant but, although seemingly happy with the arrival of her four grandsons, Peggy never made an effort to visit her daughter and family.

Chapter Eight

Richard King sat in the taxi, heavy drizzle making the night shift even more tedious. With still a year to finish his studies he reflected on his life, on how a series of events had changed it forever. First he had met Meg and despite her letters stopping completely, not a day went past or more especially a night in the bed they had shared, that he did not think of her. Since the death of his father he had become the sole male in the household and his family had become his life. The past two years had not been easy.

The upkeep on the old mansion he shared with Emma, Sara and his mother, was deteriorating and even though he worked every night to maintain it, the task was getting beyond his reach, financially and logistically. Knowing his beloved grandmother would consider driving taxi's distasteful, even if it were to add much needed funds to the family purse, he simply told her he was working part time for a legal firm after hours and Sara seemed to accept this. Her world was disappearing around her and survival had become her main pursuit. Even though she had sent some of the more valuable family heirlooms to Sotheby's, sadly they failed to raise much money.

Sara had also personally changed dramatically, her past life long gone. Meg had come into her life and through her sensuality and vibrant personality, Sara had lived in a dream, reliving and passing on old skills and memories.

159

Now she was facing the reality of her age and times, along with the financial constraints caused by the current situation, things she was unable to accept.

One evening Sara called Richard into her powder room and holding him firmly by the hand, spoke in a tone of deadly seriousness, "Richard, I am sorry about very few things in my life, except of course losing a husband and a son, but I am sorry about Meg, a young girl whom I shall always hold dear to the end of my days. I have today, with the help of Emma and your mother, packed a large chest with several items and you must promise one day to deliver them to her. Even if she is married you must still deliver them to her for me and I trust implicitly that you will follow my instructions. When we are gone, sell everything else and go to Australia and find her, promise me."

Richard remembered the conversation well. They were both overcome with emotion and holding each other tightly, unable to stop small sobs as they comforted each other. Recollecting it now, his thoughts disappeared as some customers appeared. Jumping out he assisted the couple into the rear of the taxi and drove off into the night, happy that he would earn a little more money to help his family. The long tedious hours also kept his mind off Meg for she haunted his thoughts and he knew his grandmother believed she may never see her again.

When he finished his shift in the early hours of the next morning and returned home, he found Sara waiting for him. "Richard my dear boy, do you really think that I would be ashamed of you driving a taxi to help us old ladies?' she asked, "On the contrary my dear boy, I am so proud of you, my heart bursts with pride, no other grandson would work as you do to help his family. You see, the couple you picked up recognised you from the dance you and Meg attended. He was the Lord Mayor to whom Meg was presented and he never forgot either of you. In fact, he came straight over to congratulate me on what a fine young man you had grown into. He understands the supreme effort you are making and suggested that you go to see him when you finish university. He is now the manager of a large oil refinery."

Richard was glad the deception was over but felt ashamed he did not appreciate his grandmother as a woman of the world for whom such things would never cause any problems. 'Perhaps', he mused, 'it is my pride on the line here, not hers' and determined never to fall for the trap of self-pride again. He had learned another great lesson in life from his precious grandmother.

At the start of his last year at university, Richard put even more effort into his studies. Well into most nights he sat by a small light sifting through all the information he could find in his quest for knowledge. A conscientious student, he made up for working weekends by burning the midnight oil, cramming as much as possible, breaking through the barrier of exhaustion and pushing his body beyond all need for sleep.

Three very proud women watched Richard graduate with Honours. Sara, knowing what he had endured, stood with tears streaming down her old face as he was handed his Diploma. She only had one dream, one she knew she would not witness and that was that one day her Richard would be reunited with Meg. It was to be her dying wish as three days after the graduation the ever faithful Emma informed Richard that Sara had passed away peacefully in the night. Richard buried his grandmother in a small funeral attended only by Aashna, Emma and a few close friends. A remarkable life had ended.

The following day Richard went to see Gordon Brown, the former Lord Mayor regarding employment and true to his word he employed Richard on the spot. Things began to change and with a steady income the pressure on him ceased. He was now in a position to supply food and necessities for his mother and Emma, who still massaged and bathed Richard, even in her twilight years, proving old habits and customs seldom die.

Sara had left the house to Richard on the proviso that Emma and his mother could continue living there for the remainder of their lives. Sara had already told Richard this and he had agreed emphatically to honour the commitment.

It was within six months of each other, ten years on, that Emma and Aashna passed away. A year later Richard had sold the house, resigned from his job and with no great expectations of finding Meg still single, boarded a ship to Fremantle in Australia. He had always known in his heart that closure and release from the love and torment he still suffered would only come if he gazed upon her once more. He had decided that if she was married he would cause her no problems but simply be satisfied to see her from a distance. Still loving her as he did, if that were the case he knew his heart would break but this was the path he had chosen.

Richard never looked back at the old home as he left. A new chapter in his life, long overdue, had begun.

Chapter Nine

Meg sat in the grandstand, her eldest son had just taken a mark in the 'under fifteen' school football competition. She and his other siblings clapped and yelled with joy. Meg lived for her sons and watching them learn and grow gave her great satisfaction but dreaded the day the last of them would leave home.

During parent/teacher meetings Meg had admired the dedication of many of her sons' teachers and now that they all attended school she reflected on her long held ambition to go back to college and train to be a teacher.

Paul often had to arrange crews to attend after-hours call-outs for Western Power and that day because of a ferocious storm the previous evening, he was assisting crews repair fallen power lines. Meg treated her sons to some fish and chips after the game and a coke each. Arriving home she was met by two grief stricken police officers and instinctively knew something terrible had happened. Paul had been killed, electrocuted in an accident.

Meg's world again collapsed and as she stood on her front lawn with four bewildered sons who loved their dad, she faced her worst nightmare. Neighbours, informed by the police, tried to comfort the distraught family. Twice in Meg's life she had loved and twice she had lovers wrenched from her.

After the funeral, Meg once more found herself alone but this time with four young boys to raise and nurture into men. Sons who now stoically stood by their mother, sharing her terrible loss. Meg was determined to find the inner strength to raise the boys and to give them the best upbringing possible.

Meg soon evaluated her position. Luckily the house was paid for and friends and work mates had raised a few thousand dollars, which along with her savings gave her a little breathing space. This though was the catalyst Meg needed to decide to attend university three days a week and study to be a school teacher. Returning to her old job was not practical and Meg in her wisdom decided school hours would better suit raising her sons. The eldest two would have left school by the time she graduated and their rent would help if they decided to stay at home, which they agreed to, both eager to help their mother. All decisions to do with the family were now made at family meetings.

Meg never forgot how her mother's attitude had impacted her life and was determined not to repeat such behaviour with her own children. To Meg it was paramount that they be nurtured with love.

Like all things in her life, Meg gave one hundred percent, immersing herself in the task at hand and began working incredible hours at a part time job as well as attending university. The children loved her so much they washed the dishes, made the beds and did everything within their ability to assist their mother.

The little family soldiered on, working tirelessly together. With only one year before graduating and her eldest son Garry starting work as an Apprentice Plumber, Meg again had the police knocking on her door.

165

Peggy had passed away and even though Meg had never had a strong mother/daughter relationship with her, she felt a sadness.   Not for herself, but for Peggy. Her inability to love her daughter had robbed Peggy of a relationship like Meg shared with her sons.

Garry, her eldest and Meg drove up the next day to meet her mother's lawyer. It appeared, to Meg's surprise, the home and her mother's little nest egg, had been left to her. She decided to sell the house as the proceeds would assist her greatly to pay off a few bills and allow a small investment for the future.

After the private funeral Meg drove alone to the house, her arrival bringing back a flood of memories. Entering the house Meg stood there wondering what to do or how to start. With no means of transporting furniture she felt the best avenue to take was to sell the house fully furnished and started to pack her mother's personal items in several suitcases, which she would sort out later. When she entered her old room it was as she had left it but on entering the spare room, Meg gasped. Hundreds of letters and parcels lay strewn on the bed and when she picked one up, Meg collapsed. It was addressed to 'My Darling Meg' as were more than three hundred other letters and parcels from Richard and Sara.

Meg, unable to control her emotions as a great flood of pity enveloped her soul, sat shaking on the floor for hours. Garry arrived, concerned as to Meg's welfare due to the length of time it was taking to pack her late mother's belongings. He found her sobbing hysterically. Unsure what to do he called a doctor who attended and gave her an injection to try to stabilise her. Meg, forever the tough little individual until now had coped with a life of great highs and lows but this one was too hard to deal with and she simply disintegrated. Her mother had dealt her a final insult. Never ever would Meg have expected or even suspected her own mother of such heartless behaviour.

Garry called some friends and placed the already packed bags in Meg's car, then he carefully put the contents from the bed in his vehicle. Something in them had triggered his mother's collapse and it must have been something of major consequence to have caused her such an upset. Thoughtfully he placed his mother in his vehicle and with a friend following them driving Meg's car, he drove her home. He placed all the parcels and letters in her bedroom and tucking his distraught mother into bed, closed the door, still wondering just what had caused their resultant reaction. Meg slept fitfully. Once again, great emotion and sadness had tested her resolve. It was upon waking the next morning and seeing her four bewildered sons standing at the foot of her bed, knowing she had caused them so much confusion and agony, that a great feeling of shame swept over her.

Sitting up in bed Meg simply told them the truth, all the time telling them she loved them more than life itself. She promised them she would pull herself together and that their family would remain strong, that nothing would change. Meg looked at Garry, so much like his father Paul, loyal and reserved, followed by Richard, whom she had named after her first great love, then Ian and finally Peter the youngest, all confused by and teary at what had

167

made their mother so upset.

Even though she had a raging headache Meg got dressed and tried to carry on as normal, packing lunches and sending the three who attended school, off with a hug. Garry went off to work and Meg sat down with a strong coffee to contemplate what had just transpired, however unbelievable. Meg still found it hard to believe her mother would betray her own daughter in such a way. 'What motivation did she have to carry out such a dastardly act on her own flesh and blood?' 'What dark side of her personality did Meg never realise simmered beneath her exterior?' 'Had she disappointed her mother so much that Peggy had carried out such an abhorrent act as revenge for Meg not following the script she had planned for her?' Meg knew she would never have an answer to any of her questions.

It now became paramount to Meg that she finish her university course and become a teacher so as to provide a stable environment in which her sons could grow and develop into normal young men.

Meg decided to read all the letters, although in her heart she knew most of the contents, so after having had breakfast and cleaned up she lay on the bed and made a start. She opened the several gifts Sara had sent her, beautiful pendants in small carved jewellery boxes, exquisite sheer undergarments and boxes of exotic oils and perfumes. Carefully Meg arranged them all on her dressing table along with the photo taken of herself and Richard at the ball never knowing they had made the front pages of several London newspapers. Peggy must have deliberately hid the papers until their departure from London.

A flood of old memories came back to her and though she loved Paul, had enjoyed her marriage to him and adored their four fine sons, Meg had always kept a place in her heart for Richard. Only now did she realise that old love never dies, her feelings for him had remained as strong as ever despite the many years that has passed since their sexually-charged relationship. Meg phoned the university and informed them that she had a rather bad headache and would not be attending classes that day. It was the first and last time she would miss a day, but today was special, she just had to read her precious letters. Tears welled in her eyes as Meg began the first of hundreds.

Richard had poured out his heart to her, seeming confused at first but then as time progressed simply told her of what had transpired in his life, always professing his undying love. One letter from Sara was the most distressing to Meg, it was to be the last before her death. It read,

'Dearest Meg,

It is with a heavy heart I write what may be my last letter. I know that somehow circumstances have made it impossible for you to respond to us.

Even as time went by my dear Richard never lost faith that one day you would be reunited

169

and my dying wish is that it will happen.

You are the daughter I never had and I have always missed your lovely smile and infectious, exotic personality.

I have packed a large chest with several of my most treasured items for you. Many may class some as taboo, but you, having known the ultimate pleasure, will appreciate their value. I only regret that I will never know if you receive them. If that is not to be, I have left Richard instructions that before his death he is to destroy them. They are for no-one but you.

Emma misses you greatly and sends her love.

I shall always remain your most trusted and loyal friend,

Sara King'

Meg spent the rest of the day reading the letters, following the lives of the King family until the death of Emma and Aashna. Then, for some reason, all letters ceased. 'Was Richard still alive in London?' 'If so, why had the letters ceased?' Meg sat down and wrote a long letter to him detailing truthfully her life since they parted and her mother's ultimate betrayal.

The following day after attending her classes, Meg

visited a real estate agent and placed the house and contents on the market. She had no interest in ever visiting her childhood home again, only dark clouds existed there. The house sold within a month and Meg invested wisely as she continued to establish a future and normal life for her family.

Meg always wondered what happened to Richard but having received no reply to the letter she had written and busy raising her family as well as now teaching at the local school, she simply blanked out their encounter and accepted that her life now revolved around her growing sons. Her responsibility as a parent paramount and more important than dreaming of what might have been.

Although she stuck rigidly to her chosen path, on long lonely nights in bed Meg still fantasised about Richard. It was in her subconscious mind and no matter how hard she tried, it was something she seemed unable to forget.

Chapter Ten

Richard King walked slowly, almost nervously, down the gangplank onto Australian soil, as a feeling of trepidation enveloped him. After so long, he was aware that to find Meg still single, or to even find her at all, would be a mammoth task. He determined however that he wasn't going to leave Australia until he had reached his goal. For him life would be impossible in the future, he just had to know 'why'!!

For years Richard had honoured his family responsibilities but was now free to pursue his quest to locate his one great love. He had never cast so much as a sideways glance at any other woman. He remembered well his grandmother telling him on many occasions, 'once a man has drunk of the nectar of total love, nothing else will ever satisfy'. Her wise words reflected her own marriage to the man she had chosen, as were 'a man will not stray if he is satisfied and enchanted by his lover.'

Having arranged for his vast amount of luggage to be collected and stored until he found lodgings, Richard stayed overnight in a hotel in Fremantle.

After a hearty breakfast the following morning, he caught a bus to Perth's city centre. He sought directions and caught a ferry to cross the Swan River, making his way to an address he had carefully treasured for more than two decades. The home was a quaint little cottage and had been freshly painted. It was with great expectation that he knocked on the door. A young man opened it in response to his knock and Richard asked if he knew a Margaret Jackson or her mother Peggy. 'No', came the reply, but he did say that they were renting and had only lived there for six months, which explained the new paint. Richard called next door but again reached a dead end. He learned that the old couple who owned the house had died some years earlier and the new owners hadn't heard anything of Margaret or Peggy.

Later when searching government records, Richard turned up the death of Peggy Jackson but despite an extensive search for many days he was unable to find any trace of a Margaret Jackson, either on the electoral role or in the records of marriage.

While most would have been disappointed with the results so far, Richard King had waited twenty-four years for Meg and his determination to find her was unlimited. He was now on a lifelong quest.

Upon presenting a letter from his old employers to their Perth office Richard was employed immediately. Staying in a motel was now totally inadequate so he decided to buy a small house in Perth and after settling on his purchase had his belongings delivered.

Richard felt Meg nearby for some inexplicable reason but knew it may be some time before he located her. His faith undaunted and his will so strong that no matter how long it took or what effort was required, even after so many years, he would end his nightmare.

The large chest marked simply 'To be opened only by Meg' was stored in the garage of the new home. Sara knew, if and when Richard found Meg, she would be given the chest unopened and had insisted many times that Richard was to destroy the chest if he never found Meg, knowing the contents would not be appreciated by anyone else nor would they know the use or significance of the contents.

For the next few years Richard worked five days a week and on the weekends he haunted all the places Meg had told him she often visited. For many hours he would simply sit watching the passing parade of people, always on the lookout for her. Even though he realised, like himself, she may have changed, he knew he would instantly recognise her. The owners of the store she told him she had worked in had no contact details as it had been many years since they had employed Meg and they did not keep past employee details for that length of time.

After six fruitless years, one night Richard decided to travel around Australia to check records in all the major cities, just in case Meg had moved. Perth had become a dead-end and as time passed his frustrations grew. He had called every phone book entry under 'M. Jackson' without luck and at the end of every other avenue of enquiry he seemed to hit a brick wall. Yet not even in such moments of great frustration did he even consider ending his pursuit of Meg, his first and only true love.

On a chilly Sunday morning Richard set off in a newly acquired campervan and headed north to Darwin. He had installed a work colleague and his girlfriend in his house to take care of it, charging them no rent on the proviso that the utilities and rates were paid. He began circumnavigating his way around Australia, enquiring in every small town he came to, often met by strange stares of disbelief by those to whom he told the tale of his quest.

It took him two years to reach Sydney in pursuit of Meg, without one lead that would point to her having been in any of the places he visited. On reaching Sydney he became ill. The frustration of his search and the scant meals on the road had taken their toll. He became a hit with the nurses when he told them of his dream of one day being reunited with his lost lover and many a tear was shed by staff as they nursed him back to health.

Always racking his brain for where next to search, Richard had at times considered that Meg may have left Australia, or even worse, had died.

After six long months of rest and scanning records, he left Sydney heading south to Melbourne. With each passing day now, he was becoming more despondent, his enthusiasm was beginning to wane. The heart-breaking lack of success in finding Meg over so many years forced Richard for the first time to consider that maybe they would never meet again. For weeks he searched records in Melbourne to no avail and knew that if he turned up nothing in Adelaide he would have no alternative but to return home and continue his relentless search in Perth.

One evening as he was scanning marriage records in Adelaide, Richard's heart missed a beat. He stared in disbelief at the record of marriage between Margaret Jackson and Paul Reynolds of Rockingham, Western Australia. Instinctively he knew by Margaret Jackson's recorded date of birth that it was Meg. With a heavy heart he closed the records and returned them to the clerk, his search was coming to an end. At least his torment of over thirty-five long years would soon be over.

Richard did not speed back to Perth, but slowly over the next few weeks made the journey, having no idea what he would do with the balance of his life. With his beloved Sara, Emma and Aashna now gone and his Meg in the arms of another man, he was simply crushed. Loving her enough though to wish her happiness he vowed to find her, to gaze at her one last time before deciding the next step in his life's journey. Perhaps he would find another soul mate but the thought didn't give him much joy. Meg was, and always would be, his guiding light, his first love for whom his passion had never died.

Chapter Eleven

It was a wonderful day for Meg, now fifty-eight years old, watching proudly as her youngest son graduated. He already had an apprenticeship with his older brother. She had now honoured her responsibilities of raising her boys to manhood and reflected on long ago deciding, in discussion with her sons, that it would be when this happened she'd take time off work and travel to England on the off chance of finding Richard.

Meg knew from his last letter that Richard's mother had passed away and that he was going to sell the house and perhaps come to Australia. Over the years she had read and re-read all his letters and now realised her passion for him had never waned. Her sexual fantasies still created deep urges within her very soul and she just had to know if that fire would reignite if she were to again find Richard. 'Had what she remembered all been a dream or, in truth, the reality of the situation?

Turning to wave to her four sons and to the girls partnering her two eldest, she boarded the plane for Singapore on the first leg of her journey. Old memories of her first trip abroad returned, especially her sexually-charged liaison on the voyage over. It had indeed fired her sexual passions but she never regretted it. Thinking back, her first encounter with Richard may not have been as enjoyable had she still been a virgin.

On the long flight Meg had plenty of time to think

177

about her life and of how the dizzy heights of the sexually liberated Sara and Emma had shaped the foundation of her own sexuality. Social views on sexuality in general seemed to have changed dramatically with each generation, homosexuality had been decriminalised and same-sex marriage would soon be law. These were very different times than those of her youth and she wondered what society would have thought then of women honing their skills to such a high level in order to achieve total sexual satisfaction.

Meg enjoyed two perfect days in Singapore, shopping in China Town and adjoining centres. She had to agree with the brochures that Singapore was a clean city and she felt quite safe, even walking back to her hotel after dark on her own. In fact she was sorry now that she had not given herself more time to go to Malaysia via the causeway and explore more. Although she had an open ticket home Meg had a schedule to keep and was soon boarding the flight to London. Sleeping fitfully, the journey seeming to take forever, she was happy when it was announced that the plane would soon land at Heathrow.

Collecting her luggage, Meg passed through Customs easily and caught the underground to the city. Her uncle and his wife had long since passed away and so exhausted and rather sorry she had shopped so much in Singapore, Meg found a small hotel, booked in and following a hot bath, fell straight into bed and slept for twelve hours. The following morning she enjoyed a typical English breakfast of bacon and eggs before hailing a cab to take her to Sara's old home.

Pulling up outside, Meg requested the taxi driver to wait while she knocked on the door. The old home had been renovated but the garden was as she remembered it. A young girl came to the door and as Meg began introducing herself, the lady of the house, obviously the girl's mother, arrived. On hearing Meg's story, the woman informed her that she and her husband had indeed purchased the house from a Richard King, grandson of the original owner, Lady Sara King, and as far as she knew, he had migrated to Australia.

Meg was astounded and again asked the woman if she were sure he'd gone to Australia. "Well, perhaps it was India," she replied, "but he certainly left England as a transport company took a vast amount of luggage to the docks at the time my husband and I moved in."

Upon learning this had been years ago, perhaps as many as twenty or more, Meg was flabbergasted. She thanked the woman, almost unable to take in what she had been told, it all seemed so surreal. 'If Richard had gone to Australia, why had he not contacted her?' Then reality hit, of course, no-one would have known where she was and he would not be looking for a 'Margaret Reynolds'.

Returning to the taxi and sitting quietly, reflecting for a moment, she asked the driver to take her to the London headquarters of the oil company she knew Richard had worked for. Upon arriving there she again asked the driver to wait, and realising this was going to be a good day fare-wise, he readily agreed. Meg approached reception and requested if it was possible for them to inform her if Richard King still worked there. Luckily, a middle-aged

179

man heard the conversation and took Meg into his office. Yes he did know Richard King, in fact, they had worked together for many years.

Seated across from her in the office, Jonathon Sadler smiled at Meg. "You would have to be the Meg Richard was seeking to find in Perth, Western Australia when he departed London many years ago."

A tear came to Meg's eye, "What happened to him?" she wailed.

"My dear Meg, I can tell you, as I only heard from him last year, that he is in Sydney looking for you and is not well," Jonathon replied.

"He worked for our company in Perth for many years searching for you but unable to find any trace, he left his job and as far as I know is travelling around Australia still looking for you. What an extraordinary story," he finished.

Meg was shocked. Here she was on the other side of the world looking for Richard, when for decades he had been frantically searching for her in Australia.

"I can give you his address in Perth," he informed Meg, jotting it down on a piece of paper. Holding the address in her hand she felt a lump swelling up in her throat. Finding out what had happened was unbelievable, her heart ached for Richard. Unable to comprehend such loyalty and devotion over almost a lifetime, she had to find Richard and make it up to him somehow for continuing his never-ending quest to find her.

As she left, Meg thanked Jonathon for his kind assistance and he in turn asked that she let him know when she and

Richard were eventually reunited. Escorting her to the taxi he said, "Meg this is such a mind-boggling story, I just have to dance at your wedding when you eventually find each other and I pray for you both that it is sooner than later."

Meg asked the driver to take her to the Qantas office, disappointed to learn she had three days to fill in before a seat was available.

Agonisingly frustrated, Meg walked the streets of London waiting for the departure date. At least she felt confident that soon she and Richard would be together. Somehow she felt like the young Meg, expectations of great passion gathering and the tigress within her ready to spring again, only distance and time now preventing it.

In moments of reflection, Meg found it hard to believe that for many years they had lived not far from each other. 'How had Richard felt after coming so far to find no trace of her?' She thought of the loneliness and quiet life he must have led, though surely he would have made some friends. Then she remembered that he had always been quiet and reserved and felt an even greater sadness for having ruined his life without even knowing it. Her mother was heartless, she thought, to have carried out such a horrendous act on two young people in love.

During the next few days, Meg simply went through the motions, fitfully sleeping on the red-eye from London to Perth, only stopping in Bangkok for fuel, not even bothering to get off and stretch her legs. She felt weary as the past few days had been traumatic. She felt responsible and more than a little guilty that she had not waited, but

181

then Paul had been a good husband and she may never have had her four beautiful sons.

Arriving in Perth at six o'clock on a Sunday morning, Meg didn't trouble her sons but caught a taxi after collecting her luggage. She dozed in the back while the driver took her to the home Richard had lived in for so long in Perth. When Meg rang the doorbell a young man answered, still rubbing sleep from his eyes. Before Meg could speak, he looked at her and said, "If you are who I think you are, our prayers have been answered."

"Yes, I am Meg," she said, then asked without drawing another breath, "Where is Richard?"

The young man replied, "To be honest, I don't know. Unfortunately the last we heard from him he was in a Sydney hospital recovering from exhaustion. I must say, it was the first time since we have known him that he seemed dejected and had lost his enthusiasm. I believe he was beginning to feel that his quest to find you Meg was over and he sounded old and tired."

Meg stood motionless, absolutely stunned, as if in a nightmare that would never end. Seeing her emotional state, Richard's friend ushered her into the house and sat her down at the kitchen table. He paid the cabbie and told her he would take her home later. He made her a strong cup of tea then gently urged her to fill him in on what seemed an incredible story of love, passion and undying devotion.

As Meg relayed the story, a youngish girl joined them, still dressed in her pyjamas and as she listened intently, obviously saddened, a tear ran down her cheek. David and

Jennifer Sharp both liked Richard and he had entrusted them with the care of his house in his extended absence. They showed Meg through the house and when they entered Richards's room she gasped, as there on the bedside table in a beautiful frame was the photo from the newspaper article of herself and Richard dancing, all those years ago, at the coming-out ball and neatly folded beside it was a sheer camisole Sara had given her. It was a scene from the past and Meg felt absolutely drained. Sensing her distress, David and Jennifer offered to take her home and assured her they would let her know when they heard from Richard. Meg gave them her address, but before leaving they escorted her to the garage where she saw for the first time, the huge chest bearing her name. Richard had marked it clearly 'To be destroyed if unable to be delivered' and had instructed David, if ever on the off-chance Meg showed up, he was to ensure that she received it.

Meg was glad to be home and just sank into her bed. The two sons who still lived with her were obviously attending their sports meetings. Her newfound friends feared for her emotional wellbeing and promised to phone that evening to check on how she was doing, so overwhelming was her exhaustion.

Two days later Meg's chest arrived and it took two strong truck drivers to manoeuvre it into Meg's garage. When they left and she was alone, Meg opened the chest. In her heart she knew what it contained. All the erotic figures from Sara's and Richard's bedrooms plus the elephant tusk with the carved box beneath it. A rush of memories flooded back. Closing the lid, Meg decided to leave them in the chest, too upset and distraught to consider unpacking her last gifts from Sara. Meg was acutely aware that Richard had gone to a lot of effort and trouble to bring the chest so far and to faithfully keep it safe for her for all these years.

Time passed and although Meg rushed to the phone every time it rang, it seemed as if Richard had disappeared off the face of the earth and even David and Jennifer became alarmed.

Chapter Twelve

Richard King had gone to a small town called Port Vincent on the Spencer Gulf.

Not far from Adelaide on the coast, he needed time-out to consider the ramifications of what he had discovered.

Although he had expected it, for some reason when confronted by reality, he found it hard to accept Meg in the arms of another. He was unsure now that he would be strong enough to see her again, knowing he wouldn't be able to embrace her, but somehow after so many years he still believed the impossible would happen. His faith and undying bond had been so strong that he never considered the inevitable and was now in a state of denial as he tried to wrestle with what to do with the balance of his life. At first unable to abandon his family, then to find his lifelong dream disintegrated. He found it hard to believe that Meg had never loved him and all types of self-doubt plagued his troubled mind. He became a recognised figure sitting on the rocks fishing, staring out to sea, always on his own, always polite, but hard to entice into any conversation.

Sally Henderson, aged sixty-three, had retired to her cottage on the beach two years ago, the only full time resident in the five seafront cottages a kilometre or so from the hamlet of Port Vincent. Every day she went for a walk along the beachfront, terribly lonely but far too reserved to make conversation with strangers. A widow for twelve years, Sally was still attractive with auburn hair and a firm body, having kept fit by the long walks and using an exercise machine she kept in the spare room.

It was a beautiful sunny day, the summer had been long and hot and Sally had taken to sunbathing nude in a small isolated cove not far from her home. One morning as she dozed on the warm sand, she became aware of a figure approaching nearby. Grabbing a spare towel, she sat up quickly covering her breasts. Richard had been for his usual long walk south of Sally's little private beach but due to the high tide had walked within metres of her to pass. Sally had seen this lone figure many times in the distance and now looking at his beautiful but sad features and ignoring her reservations she started a conversation.

Richard approached and was glad this rather attractive woman had spoken to him and had invited him to sit down beside her. At first he felt reluctant but on seeing her semi-naked body, long forgotten feelings rose to the surface. During the next half hour they told each other their life stories so far. Sally had lost her husband and never having a child had compounded her loneliness. Richard recognising this as an opportunity to release himself from the heartache of years of torment, and as a time to let go of the past, shared his own story, never missing a detail.

A lump rose in Sally's throat as this lovely but broken man told her of his great love and romance and of the frustrating years that followed, brought on by family loyalty and devotion to his mother and grandmother.

Sally's husband had been a good man, but on the romantic side always left her wanting, aching for more.

Over the years she had lost her sexual drive and simply enjoyed the life they shared. Now this story of great passion aroused her long-suppressed urges and created an interest in this quiet man, who she had been aware of but never seen up close. She realised now why he was staying in Port Vincent, he was a lost soul.

The sun came up and as the heat rose Sally invited Richard to join her for a swim. He replied he would love to but had no togs. She smiled and said seductively, "Well Richard, neither do I," dropping her towel to reveal she had nothing on.

Richard was unable to take his eyes off her body and gulped, Sally was the first naked female he had stood before since Emma had stopped visiting his room many years ago. Taught all his life that nakedness is not shameful, he slowly undressed while staring at the bushy mound between Sally's legs. Bemused and almost embarrassed, he tried to stop, but it was the first vagina he had seen with pubic hair. Sally also felt a power when she realised he was staring at her womanhood and became even more aroused as he stood before her naked, his penis fully erect.

Overcome with raw sexual energy, Sally approached him in an embrace, unable to stop her hand from slipping down to hold the erect member pushing against her. In a moment of madness Richard almost threw her to the ground. Forgetting all his past training, he entered her in one gigantic push, causing her to cry out in ecstasy, as years of pent-up passion exploded. Again Richard felt his passion rise and once more entered her, thrusting in and out. As Sally started to swell and meet his thrusts, he pulled her legs up into the deep stroke position and, unable to control himself any longer, felt gushes of semen ejecting into her. After so many years he had become a bit slack but started to kiss and fondle her breasts and immediately felt his hardness return. Slowly at first but now rising to his full measure he again pushed her legs up and back for maximum depth, then plunged deep into her as she rose with each thrust to meet him.

Both had been so many years in the sexual wilderness that the fire burning within them was breath-taking. Sally had never had such prolonged intercourse and with her vagina now soft but swollen, she screamed, "Harder, faster," as she rose to her first-in-decades-orgasm of shattering proportions. Richard rode her like a raging bull and once again shuddered as he orgasmed deep within her. They rolled apart, both heaving for breath and unable to believe what had happened. Sally lay with her legs spread wide, feeling no shame or guilt, fully aware it was the best sex she had ever had. If this was what a good fuck was like, she wanted more.

Richard, himself satiated, thought 'Why chase a dream? Sally was nice, no love perhaps but they both had a raw sexual energy that needed to be satisfied.' Regaining control, Sally invited him back for lunch, not wanting their time together to end. In fact she admitted to herself that she was 'hot for more!'

Wrapping towels around themselves they wandered back to the shack, chatting like old friends. Upon entering the cottage they dropped their towels and headed for the shower. Now with a sexual hunger, Richard treated Sally to the most sensual encounter she had ever had, and after drying each other off they fell onto the bed together, locked in an intimate embrace. If Sally had not realised yet that she had found a lover of extreme talent, she was to find it out throughout that afternoon and night. Richard, controlling himself, teased her in all the right places and now fully at ease with him and craving for more, he brought her to the heights of ecstasy. In hours of lovemaking, the like of which she had till now only dreamed of, she begged him to take her again and again.

The next morning over breakfast, at Sally's invitation, Richard agreed to move in. They strolled the short distance to the caravan park and packed his belongings, then drove back to what would become home to the new lovers.

Meanwhile at Richard's house in Perth, David, his caretaker, picked up the phone, relieved to hear Richard's voice. Yes, he was well, very well in fact. He had moved in with a woman after finding out Meg had married. David swallowed hard, saying nothing about Meg, assuring him all was okay and that he and Jennifer would be happy to continue taking care of the house.

David hung up the phone, made a strong coffee and pondered his predicament. Richard seemed happy at last and David asked himself, 'If Richard and Meg did meet again would they be happy?' He decided to let sleeping dogs lie and saw no alternative but to keep the whole situation a secret.

Richard and Sally became firm friends, not in love but in lust, enjoying long walks on the beach and hours of lovemaking. Richard again tuned his skills and many a night Sally's moans and then screams of delight filled the little cottage, her sexual fantasies fulfilled. Now clean-shaven and having become insatiable, Sally panted with delight wondering what great heights Richard would take her to every time she saw his erect penis coming towards her and she ached to be sated by his 'sword of delight'.

Still never forgetting Meg, Richard, after years of loneliness and thinking she was married, kept his sanity by pleasing and satisfying Sally. He plunged headlong into the relationship, his sexual energy released time and time again. Even during the day Sally would only have to bend over, or meet his eyes and his hunger exploded and he took her over the table, on the couch, on the floor and in the shower, uniting them in unremitting sexual encounters.

Chapter Thirteen

Meg decided to work part of the year as a volunteer, teaching in the outback. More than two years had gone by and there was no sign of Richard. David had promised to contact her if he heard anything and as time passed Meg wondered, since he had been ill in Sydney, if some tragic accident had befallen him. From the experience of her own past tragedies, she knew that one must keep living, so Meg made plans to keep her life interesting and to do something different.

Her family now all married and with lives of their own, she considered it time she enjoyed her twilight years. Although Meg had a couple of dates with male friends, nothing eventuated. Twice she had lost partners whom she had considered would be with her for life and the spark had just gone out.

Meg loved the adventure of living and working on cattle stations and in isolated communities. Being a woman who had always loved children, she plunged herself into the lives of the indigenous children and shared their adventures. Often she watched their smiling faces and as they were fishing, horse-riding or playing their games, she wondered what kind of a life they would eventually lead.

Never did Meg not think of her first love Richard. Now fully aware of what had actually happened, during many a long night tears came to her eyes as she thought of what might have been. In reality Meg knew circumstances had

191

prevented them from finding each other, mainly because of her mother's treachery and Richard's dedication and loyalty to the King family dynasty. Meg knew too that not having had children of his own, Richard would upon his death be the last of his family line and that in itself was another sad part of the whole tragedy.

Meg returned to her home and garden for short periods and with all her sons now married, looked forward to visits from her ever-increasing brood of grandchildren. Loneliness however drove her back to the wilderness and to the indigenous children as they continued living their dreams. Meg often opened the large chest and one day in a moment of madness cleaned out her bedroom so she could set up all the treasures the late Sara King had left her. Although much smaller than Sara's rooms, Meg still found the atmosphere erotic and stimulating, a boring bedroom transformed into a lover's nest.

Lighting some incense sticks, Meg lay on the bed rubbing herself with the essential oils. As the old feelings came back, she remembered Sara telling her that 'age is no barrier to sexual enlightenment.' Many a night Meg practised the muscle control taught her by Emma and Sara, in the hope Richard returned.

Influenced no doubt by the sexual ambience of her bedroom, Meg's erotic fantasies and libido reached new heights. The passage of time had not diminished her longing or the beautiful memories reignited by her surroundings.

Meg became so frustrated by her longing for Richard that she visited David on several occasions to double check that he had not been in contact. On the last occasion,

David was so concerned about her state of mind that he knew he would have to change his earlier decision.

Promising Meg he would try to locate Richard for her, he phoned him that evening. Begging forgiveness, he told him the full story and passed on Meg's address. David also informed Richard that the chest had been delivered to Meg as instructed.

Richard was shaking as he replaced the phone, tears welling up in his eyes. Sally knew immediately that something was terribly wrong and seating herself beside her lover she begged him to tell her what had made him so upset. Richard looked at the woman with whom he had shared his life for more than eighteen happy months and in his heart knew he had never loved her but that they had simply filled a void in each other's lives.

Going on to explain what he had just been told, not missing or hiding anything, tears welled in Sally's eyes as she realised her time with Richard was at an end. She knew he was still in love with Meg and, although he was a true gentleman to her and had taken her to the heights of sexual pleasure, Sally knew too that to try and keep him would be unfair to them all. She would miss him dearly and heart-breaking though it was, she loved him enough to release him. "Richard, I am grateful for the wonderful time we have spent together but in my heart I have always known you loved another woman. I will forever be your friend and if you marry Meg, I will dance at your wedding. I thank you for the great companion and lover you have been to me. Go, my dear Richard, to your Meg, with my blessing."

193

With that, Sally sank back in the chair and sobbed uncontrollably, she was living her worst nightmare. She knew she had never held Richard's heart and that one day she may lose him to Meg.

However grateful to Sally he was, Richard also knew, with age catching up on him, that he must end his torment. 'Was Meg a dream lost in the mists of time, or was it still all real?' He had to find out. During the night he and Sally made love for the last time and it was a sad farewell the following morning as they embraced, both shedding tears. Having come together at a time when they needed love and tenderness, the union had been good for them both and neither would ever forget the other.

Richard drove day and night, stopping to sleep only when overcome with exhaustion. The closer he came to his destination, his heart beat faster and his legs became weaker. 'Was his lifelong dream about to come true?'

Chapter Fourteen

For some time it had been Meg's usual practice to have a lay-in on Sunday mornings but today for some reason she rose early and feeling refreshed decided to tidy up the front garden. Now alone, since all her sons had their own houses complete with wives and children, it was up to Meg to keep her family home shipshape.

Kneeling in the sunshine enjoying the smell of fresh soil, Meg hardly noticed a vehicle pull up at her front gate. Turning as she heard the hinges of the gate squeak, Meg stared spellbound. It was her Richard. No mistake, it was definitely her Richard, after all these years.

"I have been looking for you Meg for thirty-six years," Richard spoke, tears welling in his eyes. Rising, Meg walked towards him and they embraced each other, both crying hysterically. Seated on the porch steps and now knowing the circumstances that had denied them a life together, neither spoke but simply sat with their arms around each other, feelings of the past welling up of a great first love that had never died. "Meg, for the rest of my days, I will never be apart from you again," Richard finally whispered as they shared their first lingering kiss since parting broken-hearted in London so long ago. They were soon to realise, as they lay naked in each other's embrace, that rather than their passion diminishing over time, it had indeed been enhanced by long awaited expectation. All that day and night their groans of pleasure wafted around the erotically decorated room. For the first few days both had an insatiable appetite and lust for each other. Never had the fire of their desire, lit decades before, burnt so brightly. Meg and Richard were together again.

It was decided that Richard would sell his house and live in Meg's. Her sons, knowing their mother's story, were delighted that at last the old lovers had been reunited and even more so when it became apparent Richard doted on Meg, attending to her every need. Richard insisted that they marry as soon as possible and Meg happily agreed. Having lived so long apart, they both wanted to bond together formally and live the rest of their lives as man and wife. On a beautiful spring day surrounded by family and friends, including Sally Henderson and Jonathon Sadler, Meg became Mrs Richard King at the age of sixty-eight. In love and beaming like a young bride, a lifelong desire and love consummated at last. Sally and Meg became staunch friends, united by their love for Richard, sharing several holidays together over the coming years and in constant contact during the remainder of their lives.

Meg still enjoyed her times in the outback helping young families with their children's education and it was on one such excursion, seated next to an author at Echo Beach, that Meg outlined her incredible story. A story so intense and far reaching it simply had to be told. Meg was eighty-four years old, still in love and with an incredible spirit, her beauty still evident. Richard constantly attended to her every need, and 'yes', still had a twinkle in his eye!

The End

BIN TRAVERLER FORM

Cut By: Dora   **Qty** 49   **Date** 07-06-26

Scanned By: _____ **Qty** _____ **Date** _____

Scanned Batch ID's

_____   _____

Notes / Exceptions

_____